Dharmapada

ODIA LITERATURE IN TRANSLATION

Dharmapada

Gopabandhu Dash

Translation and Commentary by
Dr Lakshmidhar Mishra IAS (Retd)

Vitasta

Published by
Renu Kaul Verma
Vitasta Publishing Pvt Ltd
2/15, Ansari Road, Daryaganj
New Delhi - 110 002
info@vitastapublishing.com

ISBN: 978-93-90961-71-9
English Translation

First Edition 2023
MRP ₹495

Editorial Team: Ankita Athawale, Renu Arya
Typeset & Cover Design by Somesh Kumar Mishra
Printed by Vikas Computer and Printers, New Delhi

This work is dedicated to the children of over 70 million workers engaged in the building and construction industry, many of whom like 'Dharmapada,' are endowed with infinite potentialities and possibilities, but wither away like petals in wilderness before blossoming into the flower of youth and manhood.

---

* Lack of opportunities, unclean, unhygienic and unsafe environment in which they work and live are their norm. They deserve our full physical, moral, emotional encouragement and support so that as they cross the threshold of childhood and adolescence and enter the most challenging phase of youth, they can emerge as mature, sensible, sensitive, responsive, responsible, competitive and productive adults, and play a meaningful role in the nation building endeavour.

[illegible] with them the

of youth and manhood.

Contents

Foreword

'Dharmapada' is the English translation by Dr Lakshmidhar Mishra IAS (Retd) of the original Oriya work of the same title by the legendary Oriya scholar Pandit Gopabandhu Dash, composed while in prison for his participation in the Gandhian movement. He described the theme as the outpouring of a 'lonely prisoner's perturbed heart.' It is, indeed, a touching tribute to the ultimate sacrifice of a young boy who saved the honour and lives of over a thousand workers employed for building the Sun-temple at Konark.

It is not surprising that this story and its theme has had an emotional appeal to the sensitive heart of Dr Lakshmidhar Mishra, a senior and highly respected member of the Indian Administrative Service well known for his outstanding and highly sensitive writings on the problems of the marginalised and vulnerable sections of the Indian Society. Exhortations of Articles 23 and 24 of the Constitution of India have, for him, a social and spiritual message. The human side of this story has warmed-up his heart to express his tender feelings in the form of this beautiful translation as well as the commentary.

Dharmapada is the name of the hero – a twelve-year old boy - who, as the legend goes, sacrificed his own life to save over a thousand workers exposed to the king's wrath. The legend dates back to the reign of Narasimha Dev of the 'Chola' dynasty (13th Century A.D.) who decided to build the famous temple at Konark devoted to the Sun-God. The chief planner, designer and builder-artisan of the temple was Bishu Maharana who, accepting the assignment, left his far-away home leaving alone his wife, Padmavathi then in the family-way. After the completion of the edifice there arose structural problems in the way of successfully placing the 'chuda' or the 'dhadhinuti' on top of the 'kalash' of the temple. Every time they tried, it would fall down. That enraged the king to order a cruel punishment by way of beheading the twelve hundred workers. The legend goes on to say that Bishu Maharana's son Dharmapada, then only twelve years' old, who had not even seen his father since birth, went into the temple site, had a happy reunion with his father and learnt about the structural problem which, it is said, he promptly solved.

There is a beautiful description of the gentle, genial and the heart-warming personal qualities and accomplishments of Dharmapada. There were, it seems, several controversies in the wake of the revelation of Dharmapada's great achievement and its likely effect on the reputation of the workers. The boy is said to have decided to end his own life by jumping off the top of the edifice into the river below to put to rest all the squabbles about sharing the credit for the successful solution. Speculations were rife that the workers themselves had demanded his death to conceal the secret of his success or that Bishu Maharana himself pushed the boy to his tragic end.

Sweetest songs, it is said, speak of the saddest thoughts. The story, though heart rending, is essentially a yardstick for the test of the ultimate purpose of human life. The young boy according to the author of the lyric - Pandit Gopabandhu Dash - puts at rest all controversy by his own extreme act of self-effacement to protect the life, honour and reputation of the workers.

Why does this eight hundred years old legend move us so deeply even today? Decay and death are not unknown to mankind. Indeed, they are constant companions of life itself. But some events become deeply emotive and get etched in the collective conscience of successive generations of men as long as truth is stronger than falsehood, right is might and life is stronger than death. Even if two truths contradict each other, it becomes our duty to accept both as a part of the mystery of things.

I am grateful to Dr Lakshmidhar Mishra for this invitation to subscribe to a Foreword.

20 September, 2021
Justice Shri M N Venkatachaliah
Padma Vibhushan Awardee,
Former CJI and Chairman,
National Human Rights Commission

Introduction

Dr Lakshmidhar Mishra's *Dharmapada*, is at once a tribute to Utkalmani Pandit Gopabandhu Dash and an attempt at exploring the significance of the story, Dharmapada.

His translation of Utkalmani's poem is at once accurate and creative. I congratulate Dr Mishra for acquainting readers who cannot read or understand Odia, with this classic.

For Dr Mishra, Utkalmani Pandit Gopabandhu Dash is another Dharmapada. He, like Dharmapada, had considered the well-being of the community far more important than personal well-being. He says "One sacrifices oneself to pave the way for protection and redemption of many others. The one who sacrifices oneself in essence, fulfils himself through the happiness and well-being of others. This is the eternal law of creation." He, like Dharmapada, had sacrificed his own life for the well-being of the community. For Utkalmani, as per "Dharmapada", "That life alone is worthy and meaningful which is consecrated for sustenance of the lives of others." For him, if it was necessary to sacrifice oneself for the sake of protection and sustenance of many as there should be no hesitation in doing so.

For Dr Mishra, Dharmapada combined "exceptional potentialities of an outstanding artisan with the kindness, compassion, large-heartedness, nobility and intrepidity of the character…tinged with imagination, ingenuity, creativity and skill." He further says, "A good human being abdicates all that he/she cherishes."

In Dr Mishra's "Dharmapada", Utkalmani Pandit Gopabandhu Dash is Dharmapada. His translation of "Dharmapada" aims at demonstrating this identity. I strongly believe that this translation will serve a great purpose in introducing this epic to the world during the centenary year of 'Dharmapada' i.e., 2023.

Shri Ramakanta Rath, IAS (Retd.)
Padma Bhushan Awardee,
Former Secretary, Govt. of India,
Former Chief Secretary to Govt. of Odisha
Former President, Central Sahitya Academy

References

1. 'Abhijnasakuntalam' by poet Kalidasa
2. 'Uttararamacharita' by poet Bhababhuti
3. 'Kiratarjuniyam' by poet Bharavi
4. 'Natya Shastra' by Bharat Muni
5. 'Sahitya Darpana' by Viswanath Kaviraj
6. 'Wasteland' by T.S Eliot, originally published in 1922 by Liveright Publishing Corporation, New York
7. 'Gitanjali' by Gurudeb Rabindranath Tagore, Bombay MacMillan, 1971
8. 'Sadhana' by Gurudeb Rabindranath Tagore, Bombay MacMillan, 1913
9. 'Upahar' in the anthology of poems called 'Manushi' by Gurudeb Rabindranath Tagore
10. Gopabandhu Parikrama, edited by Prof. Nityananda Satpathi and published by Pujya Puja Sansad, Chauliaganj, Cuttack-4 (October, 1976)
11. 'Utkalmani' in Oriya by Gyanpeeth Awardee Shri Gopinath Mahanty
12. 'Manusyatar Mapakathi' (measuring yardstick of being

humane) in Oriya by Pandit Godavarish Mishra published in the 27th special edition of 'Samaj'.

13. 'Pandit Gopabandhu' in English by Prof (Dr) Sreeram Chandra Dash (1964)
14. 'Political philosophy of Pandit Gopabandhu Dash in English by Prof. Dolagovinda Panda
15. 'He Sathi! He Sarathi' (O, Companion!, O, Charioteer !) in Oriya by Prof. Nityananda Satpathi.
16. 'Katha Kahe Konark' in Oriya by Dr Kartikeswar Patra published by Gyanayuga Publications, IRC village, Bhubaneswar (2017)
17. 'Konarke' in Oriya by Pandit Nilakantha Dash (1919)
18. 'Kurukshetra' original in Hindi by Rastrakabi Ramdhari Singh (Dinkar) with English adaptation by Dr Shachi Kant and Dr Raman P. Singh published by Vani Prakashan, 4695, 21A Daryaganj, New Delhi, 110002 (2013)
19. 'Sri Radha' in Oriya and English by Padma Bhusan Shri Ramakant Rath, published by Rupa & Co (1999)
20. 'Sahitya Katha' by Prof (Dr) Sreenivash Mishra, Published by Cuttack Students Store (1967)

Acknowledgements

I must acknowledge with all humility that I am not a creative writer and have no pretension of making any claim to be one. The writings (mostly non-fiction relating to Indian labour, economy, education, health, nutrition, sanitation, human rights, human bondage and human development in totality) that I have to my credit over a period of the last two decades, have been in response to the stirrings of a responsive heart which has always been sensitive to human misery and suffering from my school days. The urge and inclination to wipe away tears from every human face and provide a little cheer and joy, succour and relief together with human dignity, decency, equality and freedom have grown over the years and have been reinforced with every opportunity to do so in my civil and public service career, following entry into the Indian Administrative Service in 1964 till date.

From my young days, I have been keen and eager to read all the writings (prose and poetry) of Utkalmani Pandit Gopabandhu Dash. These have considerably influenced my thinking, psyche, attitude and approach to life. These writings are a natural and spontaneous outpouring of a very noble, devout and dedicated soul which is broad, abnegating and magnanimous, who is ever keen and eager to think, work and live for others, with no time whatsoever for self. I have been particularly influenced by his lyric 'Dharmapada' which in my humble judgment is the best among all his creative writings. The lyric was composed sometime between 1923 and 1924 when he was detained in Hazaribagh jail for his participation in Bapu's civil disobedience and non-cooperation movement. As the author has himself acknowledged with all modesty in the preface to the lyric, this was nothing but, "a momentary spark of a scattered and troubled heart." Composed in a metrical style, it is incredibly simple, colloquial, easily intelligible but intensely humane, sensitive and heart rending to the core. Every word and every verse is a reflection of a deeply perceptive and sensitive heart, overflowing with abundance of intensely humane feelings and emotions.

This is the first translation that I have attempted so far and in doing so, I have been acutely conscious of my limitations. This is because of two reasons. Firstly, no literal translation of words and expressions in a particular language, used in a particular text and specific context with a lot of inner meaning hidden therein by the original author is easy. The translator has to often derive a meaning in English which may not be an appropriate adaptation but could in all probability be an approximate or nearest equivalent. Secondly, capturing and reproducing the spirit of the original, which is a great work of art and inimitable, is an up-hill task. This is because while everything else such as tala (harmony), chanda (metre) and laya (pause) in a composition can be reproduced albeit imperfectly, if not effortlessly, human emotions which are untranslatable cannot be so easily recaptured.

These limitations notwithstanding, I made a sincere attempt to undertake this formidable exercise partly in response to the promptings of my inner conscience, but largely on account of the wise counsel of some of my close friends that such a translation will help in disseminating the profound thought and philosophy contained in 'Dharmapada' to the readers of the outside world for whom this all-time great lyric has remained inaccessible due to the linguistic barrier. The text translated into English may hopefully remove that barrier to some extent.

Keeping this sound objective in mind, I have tried to make the translation as simple, intelligible, humane and sensitive as the original even though I am not sure if I have succeeded in recapturing the emotion of the original in its entirety. Additionally, I had to struggle with a number of words/expressions like 'Niranjan', 'Nidan', 'Nirbeda', 'Gati', 'Agati', 'Aja' etc. While 'Gati' could mean salvation, it could also mean 'shelter' or 'support or 'movement'. While the literal meaning of 'Aja' is birthless, it is not very clear as to what exactly would be its meaning in the context in which it has been used. The literal meaning of 'Nirbeda' is mortification, remorse or grief but the context in which this expression has been used appears to be somewhat unclear.

Despite these limitations, I have tried hard to live up to the spirit of the original to the best of my ability, being acutely conscious of the fact that I am not a professional translator and being simultaneously unsure as to how the translated text would be received by literary critics, fans of Gopabandhu's writings and posterity.

In undertaking this exercise, I have been greatly influenced by two literary creations. First, "Katha Kahe Konark" (Konark speaks) which is a historical novel by Dr Kartikeswar Patra who is considered to be an acknowledged authority on (a) history of glorious naval trade of Odisha and (b) Kharavela, the unrivalled and most illustrious Kalinga emperor of the 2nd/1st century BC. Second, 'Kurukshetra' original in Hindi by the national poet Ramdhari Singh (Dinkar) with an adaptation by Dr Shachi Kant and Dr Raman, P. Singh.

The first provided rich historical inputs on a number of historical characters like king Langula Narasimha Deva, Maharani Anusuya Devi, Maya Devi (whom the king Langula Narasimha Deva loved but could not marry) (a prominent character which appears vividly in 'Konarke', a kavya by Pandit Nilakantha Dash (1919) who was vice-chancellor, Satyabadi Vidyapeeth, founded by Gopabandhu), Chandrika, the king's sister, who was married to Paramardhi Deva, the general in the king's army who died while fighting a heroic battle, Sadasiva Samantaray, the king's Minister and Chief Architect of Konark temple, Bishu Maharana, the chief mason, artisan and sculptor of the Konark temple, his wife-Padmavati, co-artisans - Sudarshana, Kamala, Neela, Sadananda and Sumanta Maharana, Dharmapada, Bishu Maharana and Padmavati's son and the central character in the novel.

'Kurukshetra', a masterpiece of thoughts and ideas, an epic-in-miniature on war and peace which is considered to be the greatest work of Rashtrakabi Ramdhari Singh (Dinkar) (Sun), revolves round the story of 'Mahabharat', the great epic, but is refreshingly different in terms of its treatment. It centers around a dialogue between two central characters of the great epic i.e. Pitamaha Bhisma, the grand sire of the Kuru dynasty and Yudhisthira, the eldest of the Pandava brothers. The spirit of the dialogue centers around the undesirability and futility of war which is derived from the conviction of the poet that it is the root cause of all evils plaguing humanity, a conviction originally found in 'Kalinga Vijay' (Victory of Kalinga), a poem composed by 'Dinkar' in earlier years and subsequently reinforced in 'Kurukshetra'. Like the noted English poet PB Shelley, the poet expresses the horrors and tyranny of war with an anguished heart and urges humanity to submit to the laws of society and creation (as in 'Dharmapada') and I quote the English translation (by Dr Shachi Pant & Dr Raman. P. Singh) of the original in the following words:

> To suffer woes which Hope thinks infinite;
> To forgive wrongs darker than death or night;
> To defy power, which seems omnipotent;
> To love, and bear; to hope till Hope creates
> From its own wreck the thing it contemplates;
> Neither to change, nor falter, nor repent.

In attempting the adaptation in the form of metrical English verse, Dr Shachi Kant and Dr Raman P Singh have been driven by the same impulse as the present translator of 'Dharmapada' - to apprise the English knowing audience about the seminal thoughts and ideas treasured in 'Kurukshetra', the modern epic of 'Dinkar' in Hindi. Both the translators have persevered to recreate the effect of the modern epic with a variety of rhymes that would appeal to the hearts and minds of the English readers.

I have had the opportunity of knowing and seeing from close quarters Padma Bhushan Shri Ramakant Rath (1934 - till date), a brilliant star in the firmament of Oriya poetry from my school days. He was teaching English in Fakir Mohan College, Balasore in the mid 50s (1956 to be precise) and was a colleague of my elder brother - Prof (Dr) Sreeenivash Mishra (who was teaching Oriya). I was then a student of class IX in Balasore Zilla School. By then Shri Rath had established a name for himself for his maturity and sensitivity in the domain of modern Oriya poetry. He joined the Indian Administrative Service in 1957 but continued his commitment to creative pursuits. His subsequent elevation to the posts of Secretary to Govt. of India and Chief Secretary to the Govt. of Odisha did not cause any diminution in the continuity of these literary pursuits but rather heightened them. Greatly influenced by noted English poets TS Eliot and Ezra Pound, his poetic persona that emerged from the poetry of earlier days was governed by the quest for the mystical, the eternal enigmas of life and death, the inner desolation and solitude of individual selves. His poetry of earlier days carried a melancholy touch, betrayed a sense of pessimism which emerged from the inevitability of death following life and a sense of futility associated with joy and sorrow, victory and defeat. His literary creations of later years in the shape of poetry, present a portrayal which is far more intense and poignant; they also show a progression to the spiritual and metaphysical content of human life. Transcendence from the ordinary to the extraordinary, from the lower basal levels of carnal and amoral pleasures of life to much higher territories of intellectual and spiritual excellence constitute the dominant form and style of his poetry. In terms of content, they have varied from a modernist interpretation of the ancient protagonist of love and union with the divine Sri Krisna represented through the character of Radha in 'Sri Radha', to the captivating death consciousness in 'Saptama Ritu' (the seventh season).

I am most beholden to him that despite advancing age, state of health and attendant liabilities of the family during the COVID-19 pandemic, he instantly agreed to my request to write an introduction to the text of the translation of 'Dharmapada'.

Padma Vibhushan Justice Shri MN Venkatachaliah (1929 - till date), former Chief Justice of India (1993-94), former Chairman, National Human Rights Commission (1997-99), former Chairman, National Commission to Review the Working of Indian Constitution (2000-2003) and currently Chancellor of Satya Sai Institute of Higher Learning (deemed university and a modern Gurukul) as also Member, Advisory Board of Foundation for Restoration of National Values has been my mentor, philosopher and guide for more than 20 years. I got to know him rather closely when he was Chairperson, NHRC (1997-99) and I happened to be Union Labour Secretary. We first met on 25.05.97 at a formal function for the release of my book "Burden of Bondage' (published by Manak publications, Delhi (1997)) by HE Shri Shankar Dayal Sharma, then President of India. His vast erudition and scholarship tinged with his magnanimity and large heartedness are legendary, to say the least. Like Pandit Utkalmani Gopabandhu Dash, Justice Shri MN Venkatchaliha writes and speaks whatever occurs to him naturally and spontaneously and his writings and utterances always abound with profound thoughts. His judgments and public addresses delivered from time-to-time are torch-bearers of a very illustrious tradition which represents catholicity and even – handed justice for those who have been deprived of their legitimate rights and his kindness and compassion for the poor, deprived, displaced, disadvantaged, oppressed and marginalised. He was kind enough to write deeply moving forewords to my earlier works 'Child labour in India', 'Human Bondage - tracing its roots in India', 'Truth – nothing but Truth - Memoirs of a civil servant', 'Bondage, Human Rights and Development', 'Human Rights, Mental Health and COVID-19'. Even at this advanced age and despite the vicissitudes of the most trying times on account of COVID-19 pandemic, he has never said no to a request from me to either preside over intellectual discourses and pour out rare reflections of a mighty mind or to contribute something in powerful writing which demonstrates his ever gracious and intellectually scintillating personality.

I am grateful to him for his most ungrudgingly agreeing to write a foreword to this work despite his advanced age, failing health and other heavy commitments to the family and civil society during these trying times on account of COVID-19 pandemic.

For their words of encouragement and support, I am deeply indebted to friends and well-wishers like Shri AR Nanda, IAS (Retd.), yet another devout and noble soul now deeply devoted to a study of Sri Sai consciousness, Shri Manoranjan Mahanty, former Professor Delhi University and currently Vice Chairman, Council for Social Development, New Delhi, Shri Sudhir Patnaik, Editor Samadrusti, a local journal in Oriya being published from Bhubaneswar and Shri Rakshyakar, Secretary, Pragatisheel Sramic Manch and a noted social activist.

I am deeply indebted to Shri Basant Kumar Mishra, former Controller of Examinations, Utkal University, Vani Vihar, Bhubaneswar for getting the text of 'Dharmapada' audio recorded in his own voice in a clear, lucid and forceful manner despite his illness. I am also grateful to Shri Sambit Mishra of the National Institute of Open Schooling for his tireless efforts to get the work published by maintaining liaison and coordination with a number of individuals and institutions.

No words will be adequate to express my deep sense of appreciation and gratitude to the imagination, ingenuity and creativity with which Shri Sushant K Behera, the graphic designer, has designed the twelve excellent illustrations corresponding to the characters and events depicted in the respective verses of the translated text. Before proceeding with this very difficult task, Shri Behera has thoroughly familiarized himself both with the original as well as the translated text, picturized the events and characters and has drawn the illustrations in a life-like manner which are bound to enrapture the readers who have the opportunity to go through this text after it is published.

Lastly, I do not have adequate words to express my deep sense of appreciation for Shri Kamlesh Kumar who provided valuable references, apart from attending to typesetting and formatting of this work. Needless to mention that without his ungrudging cooperation and software support, it would have been difficult for me to have taken up this work and to have brought it to a logical close in an incredibly short period of time during an excruciatingly difficult phase of human history due to the COVID-19 pandemic.

Preface

Gopabandhu Dash

I had an intense desire from my early childhood days to be a poet. I had also made some efforts in that direction at a very early stage. Regretfully, in the course of subsequent events, my life has been scattered and in that disturbed rhythm of life the desire of writing poetry has ebbed and almost died out.

'Dharmapada' is neither the germination nor the culmination of that hope; it is a momentary spark of a troubled heart. 'Dharmapada' is one of the stray thoughts which had occurred to me from morning to evening when I had been confined to the lonely cells of a prison and when I was half awake and half asleep.

'Dharmapada' is based on an oft-repeated legend of Utkal. The story of 'Dharmapada' is a crystal-clear portrayal of happiness and glory inherent in one's self-abnegation and sacrifice for the sake of one's motherland and for others (who need them most). It rests on the philosophy of every human being doing something positive which makes promotion of the highest good of the largest number of people possible, feasible and achievable.

People of Odisha have often been found to use the dictum 'liability of twelve hundred artisans versus that of one's son' in the context of application of the above principle of 'Neeti Shastra' ('Treatise of Principles'). Regretfully, however, such a fine legend has not found expression anywhere in Oriya literature so far. Besides, the original story remains unknown to many. According to the story, which generally finds expression amongst the rank and file in Odisha, Dharmapada's father Bishu Maharana himself, in deference to the wishes of the twelve hundred artisans, killed Dharmapada by throwing him from the top of the temple when Dharmapada succeeded in placing the 'Dadhinauti' i.e. 'Chuda' on the top of the 'Kalas' of the temple, bringing the work of construction of the temple to a successful close.

The above story is both improbable and also extremely unnatural as no father would ever indulge in such a wantonly cruel and barbaric act against his own son. Besides, it is equally unfair for the twelve hundred artisans to make such an unusual request (meaning thereby that it is most improbable that such a request was ever made).

It may be somewhat difficult for a twelve-year-old boy like Dharmapada to accomplish what the twelve hundred artisans failed to do but it is certainly not impossible by any count. Such extraordinary capability and genius do sometimes come to the surface and manifest fully from time to time. The story of Dhruba, Prahlada, Eklavya, Suka Muni and Abhimanyu are themes of puranic lore whereas the extraordinary genius of Jagatguru Adi Shankaracharya and Badal etc. is a subject matter of history.

Such extraordinary feats have also been found in modern times. Currently (early part of twentieth century), a five-year-old boy in Myanmar (old Brahmadesh or Burma) is reported to be disseminating esoteric knowledge of supreme God and philosophy related to religion through his preachings. Hundreds and thousands of people are being profoundly influenced by this extraordinary genius and are becoming his followers.

Looking at such extraordinary and superhuman genius, who can term the story of Dharmapada to be a mere figment of one's imagination? It is quite natural, also a refreshing coincidence that Dharmapada's advent on the scene was at a time when the art, architecture and sculpture of Utkal had attained extraordinary heights, justifying the name 'Utkal' which means the highest form of development of art.

'Dharmapada' is not an attempt to give vent to either the complexity of a literary work or the finesse of any sculptural presentation. At one time, I had thought of developing the legend in the size of a novel. Then I thought that it will be long in shape and will also be a painstaking effort requiring a lot of patience and concentration of mind. It is not possible for an ordinary prisoner like me to accomplish such a feat in the dark and empty cells of a prison where so much leisure and patience are not to be found. I, therefore, gave up that idea.

I went back to the dream of my childhood and started composing 'Dharmapada' in the style of metrical alignment. Together with 'Dharmapada,' a few other compositions such as 'Kara Kabita' or 'Poetry in Prison,' 'Bandira Swadesh Chinta' or 'Reflections of a prisoner about his motherland' were attempted and were brought to a logical close. I had derived immense personal satisfaction from these compositions during my desolate prison life. Even though Dharmapada does not carry the enchanting beauty of a kavya or poetry, far less a Mahakavya or great poetry, it is the manifestation of a lonely prisoners' perturbed heart. I will be immensely happy and delighted if the people of Odisha are inspired and motivated by the patriotic impulse of 'Dharmapada' even for a moment.

—Gopabandhu Dash

Translator's note

I have been a regular and avid reader of 'Dharmapada' since my school days. I first saw the publication in the personal library of my elder brother, Prof. (Dr) Sreenibash Mishra in 1955 when he happened to be a lecturer, Dept. of Oriya in Fakir Mohan college, Balasore, Odisha and I, a student of class VIII in Balasore Zilla school. Thereafter, I have read it several times and every time I read it, I used to feel completely overwhelmed by feelings of intense happiness, joy, sadness, the pride of patriotism and simultaneous disillusionment and despair. I used to feel transported to a different world. I also felt elevated and crest-fallen at the same time. On the whole, and such has been the overwhelming effect of going through each and every stanza of this all-time great lyric that even today when I go through 'Dharmapada', I feel 'enraptured, feasted and fed' in the words of the great German poet-Goethe (Goethe, Johann Wolfgang von (1749-1832)).

'Dharmapada' is indeed a classic work of all times by Pandit Utkalmani Gopabandhu Dash. He wrote it in Hazaribagh jail where he was imprisoned by the then colonial government between 1923 and 1925 on the charge of his voluntary participation in Bapu's civil disobedience/non-cooperation movement. The author had originally thought of writing a novel by utilising the legend of Dharmapada but later gave up the idea as a novel would be large in size, would consume a lot of time and patience and in the situation in which he was placed then, it was not possible for him to translate this idea to action.

As the poet has himself acknowledged with all modesty and humility, 'Dharmapada' is the momentary spark of the mind of a lone prisoner placed in the dark and lonely cell of a prison; it does not have the embellishment of either a mahakavya (great poem) or kabya/kabita (poetry) as is ordinarily perceived.

What then is the secret of success of this epic work which over nearly a century has moved to the core countless readers who are ardent fans of Utkalmani? Doubtless, it has profoundly shaped and influenced the symmetry of my thoughts as also my positive attitude and approach to life. The richness of the universal human appeal of the work may be attributed to many of its seminal characteristics such as simplicity, lyricism, an intensely humane, empathetic and sensitive portrayal of human characters and situations, rich interplay of human emotions, depth and profoundness in their depiction.

The secret of the success of the work, however, lies in the following few lines which translated to English from the original Oriya would read like:

> One sacrifices oneself
> To pave the way for
> Protection and redemption of many others
> The one who sacrifices oneself
> In essence, fulfils himself
> Through the happiness and well-being of others
> This is the eternal law of creation. **Verse 198**

Self-abnegation and renunciation are the quintessential principles underlying these lines. As it is said in Sanskrit, "Tyagenaiken Amrutatwam, Nanasu", meaning thereby that the quality of nectar is to be found only in renunciation or self-sacrifice and in nothing else. Such renunciation has to be natural and spontaneous i.e. self-propelled and self-driven to make sense. It must originate from the innermost recesses of one's heart and should not be imposed by anyone else from outside. We have a number of stories and fables (like the story of king Rantideva of 'Srimad Bhagavat'

Purana, king Sibi of epic 'Mahabharata' and sage Dadhichi of 'Shrimad Bhagavat' Purana) which have been woven around this principle. In all these cases, the self-abnegation and sacrifice were self-propelled and self-driven and not inspired or motivated from outside. In each of these cases, it led to (a) protection of the weak, helpless and voiceless in a given situation and (b) welfare and redemption of humanity.

This principle is the pivot around which the story of 'Dharmapada' revolves, imparting it a unique character; which, as a matter of fact, is the principal silver lining of the story.

What then is the story of 'Dharmapada'?

As the legend goes, Maharaja Langula Narasimha Deva 1 of the 'Chola' dynasty who was ruling Utkal between 1239 AD to 1264 AD, took a decision to construct a temple dedicated to the worship of Lord Sun (Surya Deva) on the bank of the river Chandrabhaga, close to the mouth of the river or proximate to the sea (Bay of Bengal). The site of the temple is known as Konark, which is a combination of two words i.e. 'kona' (angle) and 'arka' (the Lord Sun) meaning that it is a place where the Sun rises from an angle. As the story goes further, the king was inspired to take this decision and select the venue of the temple on the bank of the river Chandrabhaga for two reasons - (a)Samba, the eldest son of Lord Krishna of the

Dwapar era, who was cursed to be afflicted with leprosy, had practiced penance and worship of Lord Sun (Surya Deva) at this venue and had been cured of leprosy (b) the main temple dedicated to Lord Sun was to have another temple dedicated to the memory of princess Maya Devi (of Sisupalgarh near Bhubaneswar) whom the king loved but could not marry due to the dictates of circumstances beyond his control. It was also to be dedicated to the memory of Paramardhi Deb, who was the general in the army of the Maharaja and had married the Maharaja's sister Chandrika Devi and had sacrificed his life while fighting and winning a brave battle at Lucknowti, the capital of the Sultan of the time.

Bishu Maharana was the chief artisan/mason/sculptor of this historic temple known as Konark. As stated by the historian Dr Kartikeswara Patra, in his recently published work in Oriya captioned 'Katha Kahe Konark' (Konark speaks), Bishu Maharana was also the chief planner, designer and advisor to the chief architect of the temple. He came from a small village near the Barunei hills of Khurda (which is now one of the thirty districts of Odisha) and was chosen by Sadashiv Samantray, the Minister to the king and the chief architect of the temple. When he left home for Chandrabhaga to fulfil this historic mission, his wife Padmavati had been in the family way for four months. Six months after his departure, a male child was born to her and the mother named him 'Dharmapada' in deference to the wishes of his father who was entrusted with the responsibility of constructing a temple dedicated to Lord Sun, the God of Righteousness (Dharma Devata). Dharmapada had never known or even heard of his father but grew up with the tender love, care and affection of his mother.

Dharmapada got enrolled in the village school when he was five years old. He grew up and when he was twelve years old, was tormented by his classmates in the school for the assumed reason that he was a fatherless child. Feeling deeply saddened and hurt, he returned home and enquired of his mother about his clan as also about the whereabouts of his father. After getting to know all the details about his father, where he was working, since when and for what purpose, he made up his mind to go to Chandrabhaga, meet his father and other artisans who were at work along with his father for construction of the Konark temple. He assured his mother that he would be back before the end of the month with news about his father's well-being. After the initial hesitation, his mother permitted him to undertake this rather arduous journey. She tied a bunch of juicy berry fruits which were grown in the home garden and which Bishu Maharana was fond of. The mother advised Dharmapada to carry them with care as this will help his father to identify the son.

After a long journey on foot with his domestic pet Balia the dog following him, the son reaches his destination and meets the father. After exchange of pleasantries, the son comes to know that his father along with twelve hundred artisans is in a deep crisis on account of the fact that (a) they are unable to fix the temple top (Dadhinauti) despite frantic efforts; every time they lift the stone to be placed on the Kalas atop the temple, the same does not get fixed but comes crashing down (b) the king has come to know about it and out of intense impatience accentuated by anger, has ordered that all the twelve hundred masons/ artistes/sculptors will be beheaded if the temple top is not fixed within two days and (c) only two days are left before the deadline comes to a close. Dharmapada attends a meeting w of the artisans along with his father, listens to their arguments and counter arguments and craves their permission with all humility to attend to the unfinished task. He expresses supreme confidence that he would be able to do it. There is a sharp division among the artisans on this offer of Dharmapada as (a) they fear that the king will soon come to know that a twelve-year-old boy has achieved this difficult and incredible feat (b) while he will receive royal recognition and honour, their lives will not be spared. Eventually and willy-nilly, they agree to the offer of Dharmapada. The latter minutely surveys and scrutinises the architecture of the temple, the foundation, pillars, joints and angles from the beginning to the end and arrives at the conclusion that the center of gravity has not been correctly determined and that's the reason why the Dadhinauti or the Chuda could not be fixed at the top of the Kalas of the temple. He rectifies the defect and succeeds in fixing the Dadhinauti on the top of the Kalas of the temple. While the artisans acclaim this incredible feat on the part of a twelve-year-old boy, their excitement and joy are only momentary; they remain uncertain about the outcome of the entire process and harbour an apprehension about the security of their lives. Seeing the artisans worried and distressed, Dharmapada finds himself in a terribly disquieting situation and asks his father after they have retired to their camp, "Will he bid for his son or for the twelve hundred artisans? Will he stand by them or stand by his son?" The father is perplexed by such an unusual question by his son and remains indecisive. As a matter of fact, he is clueless, speechless and dumbfounded. Dharmapada assures him and through him the twelve hundred artisans that he is new to the place, unknown to everybody in as much as nobody is aware of his advent on the scene and nobody will ever know once he departs from the scene in obscurity. Having said this, he makes up his mind to put an end to his life in the larger interest of protection of the lives of the twelve hundred artisans who, according to him, are the pride of the land, jewels of the clan and are entitled to live a life of dignity and honour of their own. A long dialogue ensues between the father and the son, centering around the philosophy of life, transience of human existence, importance of sacrifice of one vis-a-vis protection and survival of many, futility of the theory of lineage/dynasty, importance of the clan and the community versus the individual. In support of his contention, Dharmapada shares with his father the story of king Sibi and sage Dadhichi and how they sacrificed their mortal frame for the cause of protection of the weak and redemption of humanity. While the father is in no mood to bid adieu to the son, Dharmapada remains undeterred like the rock of Gibraltar in his resolve to leave. As he finally leaves, the father falls down unconscious. At that unearthly hour, when the night is about to end and the dawn about to begin, he climbs to the top of the temple and makes a supreme sacrifice by jumping into the river and the deep sea below and loses his mortal identity therein forever.

While this is the pith and substance of the story of the twelve-year-old Dharmapada, the poet in his inimitable style has presented a narrative which is deeply enthralling in terms of language, style of presentation, depth, animation and sensitivity with which the characters have been portrayed as also the eventual tragic end of the hero.

An impassioned reader will be moved to read between the lines and would recollect the same pathos in 'Ode to West Wind' by the noted English poet PB Shelley:

> We look before and after
> And pine for what is not
> Our sweetest songs are those

That tell us of the saddest thoughts.

The story of Dharmapada as depicted by the poet is indeed sad and tragic and is bound to move any sensitive reader to tears.

Dharmapada is the central character and hero in this masterpiece. Although he lived a brief span of only twelve years, the poet has imparted an exalted dimension to this character at every stage. In his young days, he was a precocious child who was intelligent, mature in terms of mental development, speech, action and social behaviour. He is unmatched in terms of receptivity and retentivity. He has mastered both scriptural, spiritual and sculptural knowledge much to the amusement of his mother and amazement of others in the close neighbourhood of the village. He is good in his studies, kind and considerate to everybody including fellow students and does not hurt anybody on the principle of the Hindu and Jain philosophy "Live and let others live." He is no doubt extremely sensitive but does not show any violent reaction when he is tormented by his fellow mates as one without a father. His sage-like character reminds one of the saintly personalities in the Srimad Bhagavad Geeta:

Sanskrit

Adwaista sarva bhutanam maitrah karunah
eva cha
Nirmamo nirahankarh samadukhasukhah

kshyami

English

He who bears no ill will to any being,
friendly and compassionate, without
attachment and egoism, balanced in
pleasure and pain and forgiving.

Canto 12, Verse 13

After getting to know sufficiently about his clan, his father and the place where he is engaged in construction of a temple along with twelve hundred artisans from his mother, he is keen and eager to go and meet him. This is but normal and natural and also shows his determination and resolve. He is uncommonly inquisitive and charged with a spirit of exploration of the unseen and unknown. As he proceeds on his long and difficult sojourn to Chandrabhaga, his destination, he plays with the sea crabs and writes his name on the sand to indicate that he is a traveller on a holy pilgrimage. The poet has beautifully portrayed this childlike pristine purity, simplicity, intrepidity and unpretentiousness of Dharmapada in verses 72 and 73.

After he reaches the destination, he finds himself in the midst of a sea of humanity but remains perfectly at ease. The eventual union with his father brings mixed emotions of happiness and joy tinged with sadness and agony at the temple top not being fixed, the impatient, agitated and angry king ordering the beheading of all the twelve hundred artisans within two days and the deadline that was fast approaching.

Dharmapada attends a meeting with the assembly of artisans along with his father, listens to their arguments and counter arguments and craves the indulgence of the assembly to allow him to lay his hands on the unfinished task with perfect mental balance, humility and yet supreme confidence. With the somewhat hesitant permission of the assembly, he accomplishes the most intricate task of fixing the Dadhinauti on the top of the Kalas of the temple in an incredibly short time. In 'Kumara Sambhava' (Birth of Kumara or Kartikeya), poet Kalidasa writes, "Kleshah phalena hi punah nabatam bidhatte" meaning "every effort on accomplishment of results acquires a new dimension." As Dharmapada accomplishes the unfinished and yet the most challenging part of bringing the temple construction work to a close, there is in him neither any pride or feeling of distinction nor any exuberance in achieving such a difficult feat in a few hours what years of accumulated collective wisdom, dexterity and skill of twelve hundred artisans could not achieve.

When he hears from the artisans' murmurs of their apprehended insecurity that they will soon be losing their heads, while he will receive a right royal reception, he asks his father courageously as to whether he stands by him or by the side of twelve hundred artisans. He totally disowns any credit for the crowning glory underlying the task of sealing the temple top by fixing the Chuda/ Dadhinauti on top of Kalas of the temple.

This is modesty and humility of the highest order displayed by an exalted character like Dharmapada as portrayed by the poet. Seeing his father in a fix and indecisive, he makes up his mind to sacrifice himself as he cannot reconcile to the idea that the twelve hundred artisans should continue to be haunted by such anxiety, insecurity and fear (as they were at that particular moment) on the one hand and be victims of calumny and infamy at the hands of the king later on the other. In a long discourse with his father, he explains at length the importance of sacrifice of one for many, importance of twelve hundred artisans remaining alive, safe and secure and leading a life of dignity and self-esteem while contributing to the sculptural excellence of the State. Demonstrating further a remarkable state of serenity and equanimity of mind tinged with maturity and sensibility, he asks his father not to get unduly perturbed by the loss of dynastical succession in the absence of a son. Such a perception and philosophical view of life is rare and uncommon for that age. Eventually he bids farewell to his father, goodbye to the artisans, climbs the temple top and after offering prayers to the supreme creator and mother river Chandrabhaga, he jumps into the river and identifies himself with the vast expanse of the blue sea, not to be traced again.

This is Dharmapada, a character of chivalry and self-sacrifice par excellence. Even though a legend, through a powerful portrayal of this quintessential lofty central character, which is exemplary in all respects, the poet has made it life-like in every possible manner. The goodness and greatness of that sage-like character baffles description in terms of its pristine purity, nobility and magnanimity. Needless to mention that the portrayal is as deeply moving as the character itself.

Gopabandhu Dash
(1877-1928)

Utkalmani Gopabandhu Dash as a human being

In more ways than one, the character 'Dharmapada' is a true portrait of the lofty character of Utkalmani Pandit Gopabandhu Dash himself who only thought all the time of the poor, deprived, displaced, disadvantaged, exploited and marginalised and never thought even for a moment about himself. As Dr Harekrishna Mahatab, eminent historian, man of letters, journalist, ex-Governor, Maharashtra and former CM, Odisha (1957-

61) writes in his inimitable piece in Oriya 'Punyatma Gopabandhu' (Gopabandhu, a noble and pious soul): "Gopabandhu was not an extraordinarily meritorious student. Even though he accepted the legal profession as the primary source of his livelihood, it did not take him to the highest level. His contemporaries like Utkal Gourab Madhusudan Das, Braja Sundar Das, Raja of Parlakhemundi and Khallikote, Sudam Charan Nayak, judged purely from a corporal point of view, were superior to Gopabandhu. The only common attribute of all these giant personalities was their oratory or gift of the gab. Effective public speaking at the relevant point of time was considered an important attribute of leadership."

What then was the speciality of Gopabandhu for which even today, he is able to create an incredible spark in the hearts of millions of people known and unknown?

Gopabandhu founded a model school at Satyabadi. He founded a large number of social institutions at Puri. He was the founder of 'Samaj', one of the largest circulated Oriya dailies of the State.

But were these his specialities? No. His speciality was his golden heart. He could totally and unhesitatingly identify himself with people and, in particular, 'the lowliest and the lost'.

Can anyone imagine today that after finishing cooking when his hands were smeared with turmeric paste (which is of yellow colour), he could without any inhibition meet a personality of the stature and caliber of CF Andrews (whom Bapu had affectionately named as Deenabandhu Andrews i.e. Andrews who is a friend of the poor and who is known all over the country for his exemplary social work) and discuss with him on the same wave-length and same professional knowledge, acumen, and thoroughness as to how to mobilise resources for the flood affected people of a poor state like Odisha?

Can anyone imagine today that at a time when he was acknowledged undisputedly as the most outstanding leader of Utkal, he used to live as a guest, as a family member of the poorest of the poor labourer in the city of Calcutta (now Kolkata)? He always thought of the poor, worked and lived for them. He had their pulse in his fingers. Their plight and predicament were always uppermost in the innermost corner of his heart. This was the power of his heart, the breadth and liberalism of his mind and spirits and the formidable strength of his personality.

Whatever powerful writings came out of his hands, be it poetry, be it essay, be it an editorial in the newspaper founded and edited by him, there was always an easy and effortless outpouring of a heart which was natural, spontaneous, bountiful as also kind and compassionate. This was also the greatness of Bapu (Mahatma Gandhi).

Hope, faith and conviction always sprang eternal in the breasts of ordinary mortals (the poor, deprived, oppressed and marginalised) after reading his works and after listening to him. This is how when he was imprisoned for his participation in Bapu's civil disobedience/non-cooperation movement in Hazaribagh jail during 1923-25, poet Banchanidhi had come out with all the pathos and poignancy of an ordinary human being who on the departure of someone as close and intimate as Gopabandhu feels desolate and broken hearted:

> O Gopabandhu
> O, friend of Utkal
> Why did you have to leave Utkal
> Where have you left us?
> Where have you disappeared?
> Such sensitive and agonising thoughts
> fill our eyes with tears.

The perplexing question which Dharmapada had posed to Bishu Maharana, his father: "To whom would you bid: the twelve-year-old son or twelve hundred artisans?" was also always uppermost in Gopabandhu's mind and he had chosen, "the highest good of the largest number" as the cardinal and central philosophy of his life.

His search for Puranas (scriptures) and epics was only to find an outlet through which he could find a place for the love of his country. He had an abiding respect for and commitment to selfless action through renunciation (sacrifice) and self-abnegation. His placing 'Dharmapada' as the central character before the people of the world was only to plead for the primacy and centrality of these attributes which the character 'Dharmapada' represents in full measure.

In the process of sacrificing one for the cause of many, he lost his wife and left his young son on the death bed (who eventually died) to attend to the call of his life's mission i.e. rendering voluntary selfless social service all the time to the country and its poor. He was made of sterner stuff and nothing could deter him from his avowed mission. The character 'Dharmapada' was of an identical mould.

Utkalmani Pandit Gopabandhu Dash was not a sanyasi in the conventional sense but he truly lived the life of an ascetic even while being a householder. The ties of the family and the kindred could not bind him to mundane affairs. His life can be truly described as a chapter of continued sacrifice and self-abnegation laden with pathos. He was truly the 'Mahakavya' of a poet's heart. Love was the primary fluid of that ''Mahakavya', such love being the love of the nation, love of all human beings and love of all living entities including plants and animals. Such love was fortified by kindness and compassion and reinforced by sacrifice. In the tears of his eyes, there was an instant appeal for humanity. In the handsome personality that he had and in the midst of his black and dense beard which adorned his gracious personality, there was always an uncanny feeling of camaraderie, an air of assurance and reassurance for the dispossessed and disadvantaged.

Like Dharmapada whose supreme sacrifice led to the emergence of the Konark temple of incomparable beauty, artistry and grace, Gopabandhu thought, felt and believed that his sacrifice will infuse new hope, faith and conviction for the re-emergence of our national life resting on freedom, justice, equality, fair-play and empathy of one for the other. This is what made him write with all the passion and conviction:

Let my body
Mingle with the soil of this country
Let my countrymen
Walk on my back
Let all the deep holes
Which come on the way
Of 'Swaraj' of the country
Be filled with my flesh and blood
Let all human beings
Proceed on the path of freedom
At the cost of my life (if the same is required)
Let the benediction of the Lord be fulfilled
This is my last prayer (to Him).
—*Bandira Atmakatha* or *Autobiography of a prisoner.*

These lines remind us of the inimitable sayings of

a blind poet of Odisha – Bhima Bhoi by name (1852 – 1895) and are both life giving and life breathing:

> Endless is the misery and suffering
> Of all living beings
> Who can while seeing
> Put up with the same?
> Let my life go to hell
> Let the universe be redeemed.

Coming from a blind person who is not formally literate, a tribal poet who lived a difficult and painful life in the middle of a forest for 43 years and whose sensitive heart always wailed for the misery of a suffering humanity, this sums up what could be the finest and the most adorable attribute in a human being's character and personality, regardless of origin and circumstances in which it is placed.

'Kokila', a poem by the poet Gopabandhu, reminds us of 'Ode to the nightingale' by the noted English poet John Keats. It is an innocent and guileless but lovely bird which over generations has stirred the imagination and fantasies of so many poets with a sensitive heart. Poet Gopabandhu has visualised something in this bird which transcends the sensual world, which is of pristine purity and free from ego and vanity. Like the English romantic poet William Blake, Gopabandhu crossed the boundaries of the material world and tried to explore the unknown, unseen and invisible supreme truth through mortal objects.

In the ultimate analysis, Bishu Maharana in 'Dharmapada' is none other than Gopabandhu himself. Bishu Maharana eventually sacrificed Dharmapada who wanted to uphold the dignity and esteem of the twelve hundred artisans, the pride of Utkal. In a similar vein, Gopabandhu had sacrificed his son who was critically ill and lying on his deathbed (he passed away subsequently). He did so rather unwittingly as there were a number of compulsions affecting the destiny of a much larger number of people which were far more pressing and which could not be left unattended. There was an instant realisation in the mind of this saintly personality that if their destiny is left unattended, tomorrow will be too late and the rare opportunity to attend to their dire needs will be lost. This and many of his other sacrifices were directed towards emancipation of a nation which was battered by two centuries of slavish and oppressive colonial rule as also deliverance of the 'lowliest and the lost.'

Gopabandhu himself died under tragic circumstances on 17.06.28 at a comparatively young age of fifty-one (1877 – 1928). In more ways than one, his death was a personal sacrifice well within the frontiers of his awareness but he was totally unconcerned about it. The circumstances leading to this tragic event may be explained like this: In response to Gopabandhu's invitation, Bapu visited Odisha in December 1927. Even though Gopabandhu had fever and was not in the best of health, he accompanied Bapu and attended all his visits to various parts of the State. In the same ailing condition, he attended a meeting of Lok Sevak Mandal (founded by Lala Lajpat Rai) at Lahore along with Lingaraj Mishra in April 1928 (initially a member, he was later made Vice President before the tragic death of Lala Lajpat Rai in November 1928). At the relevant point of time, there were over one lakh Oriya sweating labourers (loaders, unloaders, hawkers, vendors, cartload drivers, rickshaw pullers, palanquin bearers, cooks, housemaids, gardeners, darwans, khansamas etc.) working in Calcutta (now Kolkata) under extremely exploitative and stressful conditions. He had made sincere efforts to organise them and ameliorate their plight. He had to visit them again and again to take stock of their pathetic working and living conditions with a view to providing relief and succour to the distressed. There was no law on migrant labour then and, therefore, no legal remedy against deprivation and exploitation of the migrant workers was instantly available (as now when the law on the subject i.e. Inter-State Migrant Workmen (Regulation of Employment and Conditions of Service) Act, 1979 has been put in place since 02.10.1980). On 02.06.1928, Gopabandhu came to know about a situation of labour unrest in Calcutta which was to soon erupt into a major conflagration. He had barely recovered from enteric fever and was extremely weak when he got the news about the unrest and left for Calcutta against the doctor's advice. He spent three nights in Premchand Boral lane in an unhealthy locality. His condition deteriorated; he, therefore, put Lingaraj Mishra in charge, returned to Satyabadi and breathed his last at 1945 hours on 17.06.28, the day of Lord Jagannath's 'netrotsava' which is one day before the car festival. This is how he sacrificed his life in the service of the nation and in the service of those who are poor, deprived, dispossessed and disadvantaged. As Dr Harekrishna Mahatab has very aptly put it, "Gopabandhu died on the day of Netrotsava. He could not live to see and participate in the car festival. Those who participate in Lord Jagannath's car festival should remember that without neta (a fine silk flag decorating the chariot of the Lord one day prior to the day of Gundicha Jatra), the three deities will not be carried to the chariot and there will be no car festival. They should remember that first comes the ideal and then the commencement of the journey."

Late Gopinath Mohanty, Jnanpith Awardee and an outstanding Oriya novelist of all times writes about this legendary man, his character and personality, "He was a great soul, always concerned about the misery and suffering of others, a sage who is lost in ceaseless constructive social work, the most ideal person of Srimad Bhagavad Geeta, who represented an ideal combination of all the laudable qualities of head and heart and who was idealism personified—broad, liberal, catholic and tolerant in all his thoughts and outlook on life, a person with the highest manifestation of the most exemplary character and conduct—truthful, outspoken, fearless, an incarnation of sacrifice, humility and compassion."Gopabandhu was an intensely spiritual person and a prolific writer (poet, essayist, and columnist) with a spiritual tinge in all his writings. He was one of the finest torch bearers of an old spiritual tradition dating back to thousands of years which has been enriched by the writings and sayings of numerous sages and seers which center around humanism i.e. love of man without strings backed by a tremendous spiritual force which is beyond the comprehension of ordinary mortals.

Love of God, love of humanity and an undiluted spiritual instinct as an instrument of realisation of that supernatural entity of cosmic dimension have been manifest in Gopabandhu's character, personality, psyche as also writings in the same manner as the illuminating rays of Lord Sun or as an outpouring of water from a glacier when it melts. He himself was acutely conscious of this realisation. His love of God and humanity was so natural and spontaneous that it gave the impression of a remarkable confluence of divinity, humanism and universal love. I quote the English translation of the original in Oriya in 'Abakasha Chinta' (Thoughts during a vacation) which demonstrate the evidence of such confluence:

There is no need
For you to go to temples
At far-off places
Open your eyes and see within
In the innermost recesses of your heart
Flows the eternal fountain of love
Where the Lord Himself dwells
Be pure and light a candle of knowledge
Pour out the juice of your pure devotion
At the altar of His feet
Remain wide awake
And be in action
In search of His dear pursuits
If you so wish to get the essence of religion
(Flowing from the observance of holy Shivaratri)
Convert the whole of human life into a Shivaratri
Do not miss your track
O pilgrim of heaven!

Gurudeb Rabindranath Tagore wrote in his much acclaimed 'Geetanjali' (song offering) for which he received the Nobel Prize for literature in 1913, in a similar vein though in a slightly different context:

"Whom dost thou worship in the dark and lonely corner of a temple.? Open thine eyes and see that thy God is not before thee. He is there where the tiller is tilling the hard ground and where the path maker is breaking stones. He is with them in the sun and shower and His garment is covered with dust. Put off thy holy mantle and even like Him come down on the dusty soil."

The second characteristic of Gopabandhu's pursuit of divinity and combining it with humanism is his pursuit of the 'larger than the largest' or 'greater than the greatest'. This is what has been said in the Vedas, "Nalpe Sukham Asti; Bhumaiba Sukham" or "There is no happiness in the narrow, restricted and compartmentalised realm of life; real happiness lies in something vast and expansive, all embracing and all encompassing."

In Part I of Canto II, Sloka 20 of Kathopanishad, this has been beautifully described:

Sanskrit

Ano raniyan mahato mahiyan
Natmasya jantoh nihito guhayam
Tamakratuh pasyati beetasoko
Dhatu prasadat mahiman atmanah.

English

The self that is subtler than the subtle and
greater than the great, is lodged in the heart
of every mortal creature. A desireless man
sees the glory of the self through the serenity
of the organs and (thereby) he becomes free
from sorrow.

Gopabandhu's philosophy centered around development of the human heart on the premise of good character and conduct which is catholic, all embracing and not confined to narrow and restricted religious sectarianism or bigotry. He always used to say:

Where is the need for any form
When a human being is endowed with qualities
For such a form is
Only the external manifestation of self.

Gopabandhu always thought that he could identify himself with all beings and all beings are his most cherished objects. This was nothing but a manifestation of universal love. This is how his love of man manifested itself as true love of God; it transcended all material objects and all barriers. Such humanism was clearly manifest in the following lines:

The Hindu is not born
To protect and safeguard his own interests
Every drop of blood of the Hindu
Is consecrated for the welfare of humanity.

In a similar strain, Gurudeb Rabindranath Tagore writes in 'Sadhana' (1913):

"Civilisation must be judged and prized not by the amount of power it has developed, but by how much it has evolved and given expression to by its laws and institutions - the love of humanity."

The height of Gopabandhu's devotion is to be found when he feels the proximity of a divine entity behind his thoughts and he feels the universal presence of that cosmic entity in the following words (translated from the original in Oriya) as under:

> Lord Jagannath manifests Himself
> In every tree, flower and foliage
> The heart of India
> Is as pure as Neelachal Dham
> It also overflows
> With feelings of liberty, equality and fraternity
> Wherever I may be
> In whichever part of India
> I shall always think, feel and believe
> That I am always
> Under the canopy of Nilachakra.

The third characteristic of Gopabandhu's life and philosophy was that he was a true 'Karma Yogi' i.e. one who carries out the duty imposed on him by the particular position in life without any personal interest in any particular event and performing duty as duty, without aspiring for the fruits of action, without being attracted by the attractive and repelled by the repellant, without passion or desire, anger or hatred, malice or ill will. Gopabandhu's philosophy was further characterised by the following three attributes:

- Total dedication to and sacrifice for the cause of the motherland.
- Self-restraint, austerity and ruthless Spartan discipline in day-to-day personal life and conduct without any craze for acquisitiveness.
- Every decision and action being sanctified by lofty spiritual thoughts resting on catholicity and self-abnegation

In his craze for incessant action and that too desireless action, without any personal interest in any event of life (the only dominant interest being liberation of the motherland and that of the mute millions), he was inspired and motivated by the following lines contained in Sloka 5 of Canto III of Srimad Bhagavad Geeta and I reproduce the English translation of the original in Sanskrit:

Sanskrit

Na hi kaschit kshenamapi jatu tisthati
akarmah krut
Karyate hyabasha karma sarbah prakruti jai
gunai

English

Nor can anyone, even for an instant, remain
really action-less; for helplessly is everyone
driven to action by the qualities born of
one's own nature.

In this drive for self-less and desire-less action, none mattered i.e. neither wife nor son nor any other familial or mundane link. All that mattered was the total well-being and happiness of others. Such a craving was self-propelled and self-driven. It came from within and was not imposed by anyone else from outside. He had liberated himself fully from the bonds of pleasure and pain, gain and loss, victory and defeat. Such liberation was a reality and would be evident from the following lines composed by Gopabandhu and translated from the original in Oriya into English:

> Life is full of worries and anxieties
> And is also surrounded by garbage
> And stench of the filth
> (Accumulating over generations)
> All that I wish is this:
> Let my mind not be be-devilled
> By such devilish thoughts
> Let me see from time to time
> In the imaginary and happy world of mine
> Divine beauty, mystery and grace.

The fourth characteristic of Gopabandhu's life and philosophy was his catholicity and tolerance of dissent. Religion according to him was not an amalgamation of bundles of rituals and customary practices but an inner awakening or realisation of a higher controlling power which remains invisible but can be realised through kindness, compassion and commiseration for others and 'live and let others live' principle. Viewed thus, true religion is coterminous with humanism. It unites and does not divide (as is sometimes perceived) human beings by love, mutual respect for each other's faith and belief & selfless service. I quote below the English translation of the original in Oriya which creates a larger-than-life image of Gopabandhu resting on broad, liberal and catholic thoughts which he harboured throughout his life:

> Give up such whims and caprices
> These feelings of division and discrimination
> Develop the same respect for the knowledge
> Contained in Vedas as well as the Quran
> Treat all the Hindus, Muslims, Buddhists and Christians
> The Sikhs and Jains as Mother India's children
> Mother India is the real origin
> Of all castes, sects and clans
> Let all human beings
> Identify themselves
> With one place of birth
> One cremation/burial ground
> One hope, one goal and one desired object
> Let them identify themselves
> With each other's prosperity

As well as adversity
Let them bestow their mind
On the vow of national unity
Through which 'Swaraj' becomes a reality.

It was his firm conviction that communal poison was the single most important obstacle to the goal of realisation of India's freedom and unity. On his way to Hazaribagh jail, he was deeply pained at what he saw at Bhadrak railway station and the above couplet was a spontaneous outpouring of that pained heart and anguished mind. What he had seen in 1923 was poignantly reflected in a heart-rending poem by noted Punjabi poet Ms. Amrita Pritam 24 years later in 1947 in the wake of partition of the country and the terrible blood bath associated therewith:

Fertile lands of Punjab
Having sprouted poisonous seeds
Far and near
Where seeds of hatred have grown high
There is bloodshed everywhere
Poisonous breeze in the forest
(Which) turned bamboo flutes into snakes
Their venom has turned
The bright and rosy Punjab all blue.

When Dr Harekrishna Mahatab speaks of Pandit

Gopabandhu as a person whose heart was always at the right place, that becomes the most apt description of the life and personality of this great man. Such a person always thinks good of others, works for and helps others who are in genuine need and distress; he dedicates himself to their deliverance.

Gopabandhu loved Odisha no doubt but treated the whole country and world as a large family bonded by the ties of love and fraternity. He also looked upon all human beings as the children of God as has been described in the 'Atharva' Veda.

The moot question is: how can human beings belonging to diverse faiths and beliefs, race, caste, clan, creed, sect, gender, faith, belief and ideology peacefully coexist?

The answer is provided by the Atharva Veda.

In the Prithvi Sukta of the Atharva Veda, the inquisitive disciples ask the sage:

'O, Rishivar! What is the creative force in which numerous people on our earth manifest themselves? The Rishi gives the reply, 'People living on this planet belong to different caste, creed, colour, language and religion'.

The disciples ask once again out of curiosity 'If such is the scale of difference of beings, how is unity possible?'

The Rishi gives the reply, 'Our earth is our mother and we all are children of Mother Earth'.

The disciples ask once again, 'Is this enough for unity?'

The Rishi gives the reply, 'No, there is one more thing to be observed. That is, when women and men converse with each other, they must speak sweet words.'

This principle of sweetness in language, demeanour and conversation has been fully reflected in our ancient epic 'Mahabharata':

> Speak but the truth
> But speak it sweetly too
> So that it may gracefully pervade and soothe
> And influence the mind of him
> Who hears
> Tell it not harshly
> So as to annoy
> Repel and be rejected wastefully
> Nor ever tell an untruth,
> Secret or harsh.

At one time, Gopabandhu felt that since Lord Narayan is the protector of Utkal, there was no need for anyone else to play that protective role. This is a holy land where, as the legend goes, the two divine brothers (Lord Krishna and Lord Balaram) went and fought against the king of Kanchi as the generals of then Gajapati king Shri Purusottama Deva (1600 AD to 1622 AD) on the latter's prayer after he was defeated by the king of Kanchi in the first battle and won the second battle for him. Once again, as history has recorded, this is the land which had taught the supreme values of peace and non-violence to Chandashoka (ruler of Magadha kingdom, ruling between 299 BC to 273 BC) who came and fought the battle of Kalinga at Dhauli on the bank of river 'Daya' (meaning kindness), where he learnt the most important lesson of his life, "The victory attained by the sword is never the real victory; it is the conquest of heart by love, non-violence and righteousness which is the real victory." This is how Chandashoka was transformed to Dharmashoka, the great after fighting one of the bloodiest battles of his life (where over one lakh persons were killed and an equal number were grievously injured) and after realising the futility of such war and human bloodshed (exactly the way Rastrakabi Ramdhari Singh 'Dinkar' has visualised in his inimitable work 'Kurukshetra').

The grinding poverty, extensive landlessness, deprivation and destitution of millions of famished people of Odisha, battered by successive cycles of flood, cyclone and drought and migrating outside in search of jobs (serving as 'dadan' migrant labour who are recruited on payment of advance, and indentured labour who are trafficked on allurements for mercenary gains) nevertheless pained him immensely and he poured out his heart-felt anguish in the following words (original in Oriya translated to English by the present translator):

> One who has seen in one's own eyes
> The plight and predicament of the people of Utkal

Is struck in sleep by the terror of a ghost
How many good and kind-hearted peasants
Are deprived of two square meals a day
Those who fought once as brave Paika warriors
Have been reduced
To the stage of beggars on the streets
Starved, emaciated and reduced to bones
They cannot easily lift themselves
Whatever they earn by the sweat of their brow
Is expropriated
By the blood thirsty Zamindars and money lenders
(They) are lashed and drained out by the latter
Driven by the pangs of hunger
They desert their hearth and home
Reducing the village to a cremation ground
Neither the Vedic hymns
Nor the sweet symphony of Srimad Bhagavat
Reverberate through the assembly of the village (as before)
Where have they disappeared?
The quest for religion and truth
The eternal longing of human heart
For serenity, peace and bliss.

Gopabandhu was a diehard optimist and with hope, faith and conviction in the innermost corner of his heart stirred by divinity, he wistfully longed for better days to come for the nation, State and the people:

> O, my dear brothers and sisters of Utkal!
> Do not grieve
> Do not give up hope
> By looking at the portrait
> Of today's misery and suffering
> (For) Joy and sorrow, light and darkness
> Follow each other
> Like a wheel
> They oscillate around human lives
> Like pairs of opposites
> Now is the turn of light after darkness
> It is the light of 'Swaraj' (self-rule)
> Which will pervade soon
> The hearts and minds of our countrymen
> Arise and awake
> Before it is too late.

In his prayer to the Lord, he seeks the redemption and deliverance for the people of Utkal in the following words:

> O Lord!
> Endow the children of Utkal
> With a virile strength
> Bless the trees of Utkal
> To be laden with juicy fruits
> Let the streams of Utkal

Overflow with sacred lives
Let the gardens of Utkal
Get embellished with divine flowers
Let the Sun of fame
Emerge in the eastern firmament
In the sky of Utkal
Let the beautiful Nature of the land
Adorn itself with a new frame.

'Abakasha chinta' (Thoughts during a vacation)

He never stood for an exclusive Utkal but always desired and prayed that the State identifies itself with the waves of struggle for national freedom under the leadership of Bapu:

O Lord !
In the fierce battlefield
Of this universe
Let the poor children of Utkal
Not lag behind
Let the streams of thought
Flowing in Utkal
Merge in the wave of
Pan-Indian Unity
Let this be your command.
—English translation of *Abakash Chinta* or
Thoughts during a vacation

Ananta Patnaik, a noted poet of Odisha describes Gopabandhu as incarnation of humanism, a true embodiment of what a good human being should be – a combined beautiful image of renunciation and service. According to yet another noted poet – Dr Mayadhar Mansingh, Gopabandhu was not a human being of flesh and blood but a divine entity who descended from heaven to earth for some time to the good fortune of the people of Odisha. But differing from Dr Mansingh and agreeing with Shri Patnaik, poet Radhamohan Gadnaik describes Gopabandhu as a human being who truly identifies himself with all human beings but more particularly with those who are suffering for no fault of theirs:

> He was truly a man and not a god
> He lived for human beings
> He fought for human beings
> For those who are aggrieved and oppressed
> Who are soaked in misery and suffering
> He could feel their emotions
> And breathe their joy and pain.
> —*Mandir O Samadhi*

Gopabandhu as a poet

Gopabandhu's perception of poetry and the importance of being a poet is to be found in a letter published in the journal 'Satyabadi', founded and edited by him (1915-21), "The country will be redeemed of its curse if a true poet is born. A true poet is the real foundation of true people's power. National life flows from that spring and floods the nation. Literature always provides a true ideal before the nation. That ideal moulds the national character and aspiration and these get fully reflected in literature."

Mathew Arnold (1822-1888), English Victorian poet, literary and social critic has termed literature as the lamp of life implying thereby that whatever is true of life will constitute the soul of literature for all time to come.

The literature (prose and poetry alike) created by Gopabandhu in a short span of about two decades is largely true of what Mathew Arnold had written about it one century earlier; it is characterised by a number of striking features such as:

To start with, his search for history and characters of historical antiquity is a search for love of his country, for generating work related inspirational thoughts and for instilling respect for one's duty, dignity, nobility, thoughts, judgment, confidence and strength.

Secondly, he is what his literary creations represent and unfold. One is a mirror-like reflection of the other.

There is not a trace of sugar coating or window dressing. Life and poetry get intertwined by a rare bond of friendship. There is a remarkable synergy of the practical with the ideal. His literary works are a powerful medium for resurrection of the healthy tradition of the past, for resuscitating a servile and dying nation, being suffocated by two centuries of colonial misrule and for imparting it speed, dynamism, momentum, strength, virility and large-heartedness.

Thirdly, as a truly creative person he does not get circumscribed by ties or strings. He transcends the limitations of nativity, home, family, the place of origin, faith, belief and ideology. To put in his own words, "Through serving Utkal, we will serve India and the world. Through the strings of Utkal Veena (a musical instrument) we will listen to the murmurs of the voice of the universal man. True nationalism is never dry, lifeless and actuated by selfish interests. It is not founded through acquisition of kingdoms and shedding avoidable human blood but on equality, fraternity and freedom."

Fourthly, he was truly a poet of 'Aam Aadmi' or 'common man'.

His poetry was dedicated to those

- Who plough the land
- Who sow, de-weed and transplant tender plants and harvest the crops
- Who water the garden

- Who weave cloth and stitch garments
- Who manufacture salt
- Who collect hides and skins
- Who work as tanners and flayers
- Who load and unload goods
- Who drive a cart loaded with merchandise
- Who work as hawkers, vendors, beedi rollers/ labellers/ packers and incense stick makers
- Who work as sewer workers and scavengers
- Who row boats/rafts

and such other categories and sub-categories; human beings entitled to the same inalienable human rights resting on respect for their dignity, decency, equality and freedom, but who, because of the peculiar circumstances in which they are born and placed, in which they work, live and grow, are not aware of their own strength and weaknesses vis-a-vis those of their adversaries and who know not what they ought to know and do not know what they do not know.

According to him, the soul of a nation lives through them, even if they may be poor, ignorant or illiterate. They are the children of nature - simple, hospitable and guileless. They sing, dance, rejoice and mourn. The songs composed by them in their native dialect are the finest outpourings of an unsullied heart, conveying a remarkable depth and intensity of human spirit.

Gopabandhu had poured out the fullness of his heart and abundance for his love and compassion for the 'Aam Aadmi'. He lived for them, worked for them and died for them.

Fifthly, he was passionately committed to the love of Nature. There are a large number of specimens of his poetry demonstrating such love of Nature. I would like to reproduce the English translation of one such specimen from 'Kara Kabita' (poetry written in a prison) which brings out the fullness of his heart along with his love of nature:

The waves dance
With the touch of the Moon
The lotus unfolds
With emergence of the bright rays of the Sun
Human heart identifies itself
With the Supreme Creator
Who is also the Supreme Lord of the heart
It dances with supreme elation
Emerging from universal benediction
The mountain, ocean, river, Sun and Moon
Will embrace and kiss me with unbounded love
The earth will float
On the crest of waves of the love of my heart
The entire universe will be my love's basket.

This is reminiscent of what Viswakabi Gurudeb

Rabindranath Tagore wrote:

> The mass of waves of my heart
> Swiftly move through the veins of my body
> That heart rushes towards
> A universal expedition and conquest
> That heart dances
> With an incomparable pause, metre and rhythmic harmony.

Sixthly, unlike Radhanath Ray, an eminent contemporary poet in whose poetry emotion occupied a dominant note and such emotion was embedded in characters which were not indigenous but mostly imported, Gopabandhu was a poet dedicated to action. His action may be tinged with emotion but remains nevertheless the central element in his poetry which was primarily dedicated to a call for purposive and meaningful action. Be it liberation of the motherland from the foreign yoke, be it liberation of the people of Utkal from the curse of poverty, illiteracy and natural calamities (flood, cyclone, drought), be it replacement of rancour, jealousy, vanity, ego hassles, intolerance, discrimination, cruelty, violence and bondage by tolerance, large-heartedness, equality, justice, peace and harmony, his call for action to the countrymen (including people of Odisha) was clear, unambiguous and highly motivational and touched the finer chords of the human heart of one and all.

Seventhly, in terms of political economy, good governance, how a ruler should be in day-to-day action and conduct and promotion, protection and preservation of human rights resting on the foundation of respect for human dignity, decency, equality and freedom, he was clear and uncompromising in his perception and judgment:

If royalty is coterminous with
Total wellbeing of subjects,
Why should the latter
Be victims of such serious abuse,
When in the name of politics
Values and principles are thrown to the winds?
There can never be principled politics
Where are the sagacious rulers in such politics?
Except the rule by the officialdom
Which wrecks havoc
On the peace and happiness of subjects.
The ruler rules pretentiously
In the name of religion,
Peace and happiness of subjects
Converting it to a blasphemy
At the sweet will and pleasure
Of a group of (obedient) minions.
Freedom is man/woman's birthright
Freedom of expression and movement
Freedom of assembly and existence

In these four pillars of freedom
Is embedded stability of human society.
—Extract from *Kara Kabita* or
Poetry composed in Prison

And finally, Gopabandhu as a poet clearly perceived that an eternal conflict was going on between human beings who are selfish, narrow minded, vindictive, full of vanity and arrogance on one side and the universal man who is endowed with the noble instincts of liberty, equality, fraternity, love and compassion. He clearly perceived that the universal self which is lying hidden behind every mundane self seeks an enlarged universal life in place of the narrow and restricted ambit of a mundane existence. The poet drew inspiration and strength for his universal man from the following lines of the Vedas:

Sanskrit

Tasmat Baibidwan
Purusham Idam
Brahmeti Manyate

English

That person is truly learned who accepts
every man as a manifestation of the
'Brahman' or 'Supreme Spirit'.

The importance of humanism and universalism and the influence they exert on the human heart have been brought out by Gurudeb Rabindranath Tagore in 'Panchabhut' with a lot of sensitivity:

'We are inclined to think, feel and believe that those 'dumb, mute and expressionless' sections of the society who are devoid of social recognition, who cannot adequately articulate themselves since they are fastened by an unclean cover (of superstitions, blind faiths and beliefs and obscurantist practices), who are not well aware of themselves, who meekly put up with human misery, suffering and pain deserve a fairer deal from us. That deal lies in making them feel that they are one of us and through our literary creation we need to provide them the light of life.'

Further in 'Patradhara Prabhas,' Gurudeb Tagore wrote:

'We need to make sincere efforts to bring to our midst that great (universal) man. We need to realise through him the eternal truth. The trio i.e. knowledge, love and (dedicated) action constitute the source of that truth. We need to give up our vanity and ego so that we may through the touch of that great soul (the universal man) realise the true nectar of life.'

Central thoughts centering round, 'Dharmapada'

As has been said earlier, the beauty of literary creations of Radhanath Ray, an eminent contemporary poet, is contained in characters which are not indigenous but largely imported whereas the literary creations of Utkalmani Pandit Gopabandhu Dash are true to life. They revolve around local legends and the life of the 'Aam Aadmi' (common man) in a local setting and therefore, are all encompassing and universal.

Both 'Dharmapada' of Gopabandhu and 'Konarke' of Pandit Neelakantha Dash, an eminent teacher, historian and creative writer of the Satyabadi era were a challenge to Radhanath Ray's importation of foreign elements.

'Dharmapada' is a rare jewel among all the literary creations of Gopabandhu; it is also a jewel in world literature although it has remained inaccessible to a large number of lovers of literature in the West due to the linguistic barrier.

'Dharmapada's central thoughts center around the following:

- Harness local legends and Puranic/historical characters of antiquity for the richness of human appeal which they represent and respect for the dignity, decency, equality and self-esteem infused into those characters which constitute the theme of the legends; these characters and the qualities they represent are expected to inspire and motivate the rest of the denizens in human society.

- Introduce the element of self-abnegation, renunciation and sacrifice of one for the survival, sustenance and well-being of many as opposed to acquisition of selfish interests through highly objectionable means such as deceit, fraud, expropriation, vilification, character assassination and the resultant dehumanisation.
- Establish a warm and humane relationship with all human beings within the human society.
- Establish total identification of self with all the characters in the literary creation as an artist does in any other artistic creation (music, dance, drama, films etc.)
- Establish felicity of natural and spontaneous expression in one's mother tongue.

'Dharmapada', as a combination of multiple rasas or emotions

Judged by all standards, Gopabandhu's 'Dharmapada' is a unique literary creation in terms of subject matter, style of presentation, lyricism, powerful portrayal of emotions and richness of universal human appeal. It is also a remarkable confluence of batsalya rasa (filial love related emotion), biraha rasa (emotion related to separation of self from near and dear ones), karuna rasa (emotions related to pathos or sadness overwhelming one's life), beerjya rasa (emotion related to valour) and bhakti rasa (emotions related to devotion).

A moot question may be raised as to what is rasa or emotion. Rasa or emotion is an intense feeling of the human mind. Bharat Muni writes in 'Natya Shastra' about rasa:

> 'Nahi Rasat Rute
> Kaschit Artha Pravartate
> Tatra Bibhabanubhava
> Byavichari Sanjogat
> Rasa Nispatti.'

Translated to English, it would mean:

'There is nothing else which can be introduced (in literature) without rasa. The rasa's origin may be traced to a portrayal of human anxiety, dignity and transgression of good conduct.'

Viswanath Kaviraj, author of 'Sahitya Darpan' writes 'Bakyam Rasatmakam Kavyam' meaning 'Sentences adorned with rasa make a kavya.' He further writes: 'Karuna Dabati Rase Jayate Jat Paramam Sukham' meaning 'Karuna rasa gives birth to a rare delight.' Kesav Mishra, an authority on the ornamentation theory in literature has depicted rasa as the soul of kavya. Shri Surendranath Dasgupta, a well-known literary critic, has said and I translate the original in Bengali into English: 'Not only streams of emotions flow through a kavya but as they flow, the brilliance of truth is manifested in every wave of the stream by new rays of the bright Sun.'

According to the Greek philosopher Aristotle, 'rasa' is nothing but emotional delight. Noted English poet William Wordsworth brings out the importance of human emotions in life through creative literature:

> "Thanks to the human heart
> By which we live
> Thanks to its tenderness
> Its joys and fears."

In the preface to 'Dharmapada', Gopabandhu wrote, 'Dharmapada' is a momentary spark of a lonely prisoner cast inside a desolate prison cell. The poet has been too modest to acknowledge that 'Dharmapada' is decidedly the finest outpouring of a sensitive heart. Viewed in that sense, as a literary creation surcharged with emotions, it is a masterpiece. Such a categorisation is quite apt and it corresponds to what Gurudeb Rabindranath Tagore has written about such sensitive hearts in 'Upahar' which finds place in his anthology of poems called 'Manushi':

Into the innermost recesses of human mind
The waves of the universe strike off and on
That heart alone is sensitive
Which responds to these waves
And reverberates them
Throughout the universe
That heart alone is sensitive
Which does not have time
For food, sleep and rest.

In one of his poems captioned 'Kabita', Gopabandhu has referred to such a person who is charged with pure emotions:

"A poet's exterior
Abounds with pure simplicity
His inner mind
Is flooded with divine emotions
While ordinary mortals
Get fascinated
By external forms
Truly creative persons
Are immersed
In the emotions of the inner self."

Rasa, therefore, is essentially an experience of emotion; such emotion gives birth to a rare joy. It is truly a sensitive mind which can dive deep into that ocean of emotion. When that happens, a rare bond is established between the emotions portrayed in the literature concerned and the sensitive reader.

'Dharmapada' very appropriately can be said to be a conveyer belt of multiple rasas or emotions such as those related to filial love and affection, pangs of separation of self from near and dear ones, poignancy of pathos, devotion and valour.

Filial love and affection come out in the very beginning of 'Dharmapada' in abundant measure. Dharmapada was four months old in the womb of his mother when Bishu Maharana, the sculptor and his father left for Chandrabhaga to work for construction of the Sun temple. Dharmapada was born six months later. He, therefore, neither knew nor heard about his father who was away from home for twelve long years. He was nurtured by his mother who poured out the best of her filial love, care and affection, while pining all the while for her husband. The vatsalya rasa or the emotion related to filial love and affection has come out in an abundant measure as would be evident from the following verses:

If there are tears in your eyes
O, my dear child!
If you do not unfold

What has happened;
(Either in the classroom or outside)
Don't you know
That thunder will pierce me
And I would fall down
As good as dead. **Verse 17.**

She further continued:

I have spent this desolate life
So long and so far
Only by looking at your lovely face;
O, the moon of my clan
You are like a garland
Around the neck of a begging woman,
Please share with me
Whatever has happened
And what is tormenting you. **Verse 19**

Separation of self from near and dear ones is always extremely painful; it is all the more painful when there is a remote possibility or uncertainty about re-union in the foreseeable future. Such emotions known as 'Biraha rasa' have been depicted with utmost pathos when Dharmapada's mother narrates the plight of her desolate life (in the absence of Dharmapada's father):

Since the day your father left home
And departed for a distant land,

I have been haunted
Day-in and day-out
By his sweet memory
As also by the pangs of separation.
For long twelve years
Passage of one day for me
Appears to be the end of a millennium;
Day after day and month after month
I pine for his company
And wistfully long his return.
I am drained of blood
And unable to breathe. **Verse 42**

When the twelve-year-old Dharmapada bids farewell to his father, having made up his mind to sacrifice himself for the sake of the life, dignity and esteem of the twelve hundred artisans, it generates an emotion or karuna rasa which in terms of pathos is without an equal. This comes out when Bishu Maharana, the father asks Dharmapada with all the anguish of his heart:

Where do you want to go, O, my son!
Would you remain safe and sound?
Would you remain alive in flesh and blood?
If you remain alive,
Who knows when
We shall meet again
Please do not hide

But unfold, O, my dear!
What is your true intention? **Verse 163.**

The element of pathos or karuna rasa reaches its climax when Dharmapada finally leaves and the father being unable to bear the pangs of separation falls down unconscious. This has come out clearly and forcefully tinged with a lot of melancholy in the following lines:

Having said this
Dharmapada took particles of dust
From his father's feet
And smeared his forehead (with the same).
The old man is speechless,
Being overwhelmed with sadness
Tears trickled down from his eyes
And overflowed his cheeks;
The old man gave his last kiss
On the face of his son
As a sign of his silent bliss. **Verse 203**

The son departed
And the father
Unable to bear
The pangs of separation
Fell down unconscious
Writhing in physical and mental anguish. **Verse 204**

The above lines fully correspond to the spirit of the following lines in the third canto of 'Uttara Rama Charita' by the noted Sanskrit poet Bhababhuti.

Sanskrit:

Dalati hrudayam shokodbegat
Dwidha na tu vidhyate
Bahati bikalah kayo
Moham na munchati chetanam
Jwalayati tanum antar dahah
Karoti na bhasmasat
Praharati bidhir marmachhedi
Na kruntati jeebitam.

English:

My heart is rent due to anxiety and sorrow
but it does not get torn to pieces. My
body is motionless but is not devoid of
consciousness. My body burns due to inner
mental agony but it does not get reduced to
ashes. My cruel and heartless fate is lashing
my heart and other vital parts of my body
but does not take away my life in its entirety.

These soul-stirring lines speak of the unspeakable anguish and pain experienced by Lord Shree Ramachandra, king of Ayodhya by the most painful separation from his beloved wife Sita Devi.

Noted Sanskrit poet and playwright Kalidasa in *Abhijnanamsakuntalam* has portrayed a similar anguished state of body and mind of sage Kashyap when his adopted daughter Shakuntala departs from his ashram for her husband's (Dushyanta) home:

Sanskrit

Jashyatyadya shakuntaleti hrudayam
sampustam utkanthaya
Kanthah stambhitah baspabruttikalusam
chintajadam darshanam
Baiklabyam mama tabat idrusam idam
snehat aranyoukasa
Peedyante gruhinah katham nu tanayat
bishleshah dukhai nabai

English

At the very thought that Shakuntala is to go
away today, my heart is smitten with grief,
my throat is choked owing to flow of tears
being suppressed and my sight is heavy on
account of anxiety. Such (so great) indeed
(through affection for Shakuntala) is this
affection of one that dwells in a forest; how
much then must householders be tormented
by the fresh (inexperienced) pangs of
separation from their daughters?

The valour or 'beerjya rasa' comes out clearly and forcefully at a number of points in 'Dharmapada'. It manifests fully when Dharmapada stands up and speaks to the assembly of artisans with strength, courage and confidence tinged with a lot of humility that he is quite capable of sealing the temple top if given the permission and an opportunity to do so. It comes out once again when the twelve hundred artisans suffer from a sense of fear and insecurity that they will be beheaded while Dharmapada will receive royal reception from the king. Dharmapada is rather peeved by such faint-heartedness of the artisans and his exalted character stands out in the face of such weak and demeaning character of the artisans. He holds them in high esteem, stands for their life, dignity and esteem and urges them not to lose heart but feel fully safe and secure as he will disappear from the scene in no time. This is how his lofty character and self-abnegating personality stands out in the open:

> Of what value is that name
> And all the honour associated (therewith),
> If the twelve hundred artisans
> Representing twelve hundred petals
> Would wither away in wilderness
> Before blossoming to the flower
> Of their full fame. **Verse 137**

Nobody knows my name here
Nobody will ever know
Since I am a total stranger;
Before the night ends
And the day dawns
I shall carve out my own destiny
In my own hands and in my own way. **Verse 142**

Dharmapada views the entire sequence of events in a somewhat philosophical vein thus:

The world is an illusion
Everyone here is deluded,
No one knows
Who is the father
And who is the son;
That life alone
Is worthy and meaningful,
Which is consecrated
For sustenance of the lives of others
The most precious object in God's creation. **Verse 148.**

In the following lines, Dharmapada dispels certain illusions or ill-perceived notions associated with dynasty and how action and conduct of individuals should be judged and recorded in the history of mankind while conveying to his father in no uncertain terms about his resolve to sacrifice himself for the survival of others:

O, father!
Life and death follow each other
(Like day and night)
In a ceaseless link.
For certain is death for the born
(As certain is birth for the dead);
They follow each other
Rather incessantly without any break. **Verse 164**

Dharmapada's distaste for recognition vis-a-vis his respect for the dignity and self-esteem of the twelve hundred artisans is clearly demonstrated:

What ghastly picture
Future history will paint,
In what colour and brush
That I would be walking
In the royal Court,
With 'saree' and 'sherpa'
Tied to my head as a recognition on one side
And my proud ancestors
Torch bearers of a lofty tradition
Will be put to death on the other side. **Verse 173**

The following lines to demonstrate Dharmapada's complete disenchantment with the traditional way of looking at dynasty and dynastical succession:

You may, O, father!
Be thinking
That how without me
Our dynasty will be protected;
Please think for a while
Which dynasty has remained permanent on earth
And what purpose has it served? **Verse 186**

So many good human beings, O, father!
Have come and departed
Having achieved the unachievable,
They have perished with the passage of time
Where is their dynasty?
All that remains
And all that is remembered
Is only their work and reputation
What they have left behind
On the sands of time. **Verse 197**

The spirit of such disenchantment is reinforced further from the following lines:

One qualifies to be called a true hero
Who lawfully discharges the duty
That falls to one's lot

With courage and valour;
History has recorded
Many such heroic exploits
Like Lord Shree Ramachandra, the warrior
Who built a bridge across the Indian ocean. **Verse 201**

'Dharmapada' and 'bhakti rasa' or 'devotion related emotion'

The ninth chapter of 'Dharmapada' from verse 211 to verse 227 is the finest and the best in this all-time great lyric which, as observed earlier, is tinged with filial love (vatsalya rasa), separation of self from near and dear ones (biraha rasa), pathos (karuna rasa), valour (beerya rasa) and finally devotion (bhakti rasa). This chapter confirms that Gopabandhu was a bhakta kabi (devotional poet), a prakruti kabi (Nature's poet), a rastra kabi (a national poet); he was also truly a viswa kabi or universal poet. The great universal being, the integration of an individual's body, mind and soul with the universal self, the universality of God, the supreme creator who is eternal, immanent and transcendent and the rhythm of universal music are all fully manifested in these seventeen verses of this chapter.

It has been said by many impassioned observers that if a reader, keenly interested to study Gopabandhu, ignores all his writings and concentrates only on these seventeen verses in the ninth chapter of 'Dharmapada', he won't regret but instead, he/she would be transported to a rare world of divine beauty, joy, peace, serenity and bliss as they constitute the core, the very quint-essence of 'Dharmapada'.

This chapter brings out the following clearly, lucidly and forcefully:

- God is formless, spotless, pure and free from passion and senses.

- He is the supreme 'Brahma', the primary cause of creation, all pervasive and all encompassing (covering all movable and immovable objects of creation).
- He is the fountainhead of kindness, compassion and magnanimity.
- He is the refuge of the helpless and shelter-less who are in distress.
- He is infinite and unbounded, has no beginning and no end, no ins and no outs.
- He is the one on whom the entire universe rests and he creates and sustains the universe.
- He manifests through all stars and planets. All objects of creation such as land, water, air, light, sound, rivers, forests and mountains derive their strength from him for their sustenance.

All these come out in the form of a prayer offered by Dharmapada before he sacrifices himself by jumping from the temple top into the river Chandrabhaga and the sea down below:

> O, my Lord!
> Your glory is infinite
> It has no beginning and no end
> Your beauty is incomparable.
> You are formless and yet visible
> In every layer and sub-layer of the earth.
> Your magnificent love and compassion

Weave themselves into every movable and immovable
Object of the universe. **Verse 221**

O, my Lord!
Higher than the highest
Greater than the greatest
You are beyond near and far, intimate and alien,
I pray you, O my Lord,
Please provide a little refuge
To me in the dust of your glorious feet;
Let your grand desire be fulfilled
Through this ordinary mortal
Victory to you, O, Lord of the Universe." **Verse 224**

The character 'Dharmapada' combined in him exceptional potentialities of an outstanding artisan with the kindness, compassion, large heartedness, nobility and intrepidity of the character of an adult (which is somewhat inconceivable for his age) tinged with imagination, ingenuity, creativity and skill. He had the uncanny insight and ability to correctly perceive the law of Nature and the law of creation, how the concept of dynasty is abhorrent to a rational and civilised mind, how being father and son are coincidental/incidental, how blind attachment or infatuation of one for the other including that of the father for the son does not take one to great heights but instead, makes life and human relations narrow and compartmentalised and brings a lot of pain, how sacrifice of one for a good, noble and justifiable cause could promote survival, evolution and advancement of many and how all living beings derive their inspiration and motivation from that unseen supernatural power, who makes day and night, whose power creates the earth, the sky, all celestial beings, all plants and animals and who at the same time radiates our minds with the dazzling light of an eternal consciousness that moves and exists in an unbroken continuity with the outer world.

Dharmapada rightly discarded the concept of dynasty which in ordinary parlance refers to succession of a monarch of the same family or of members of any other powerful family or connected group. As a concept and practice, it is irrational and abhorrent for the following reasons:

- The person chosen for succession may or may not be as good, virtuous/meritorious and of the same exalted character as the person (king) by whom he/she is chosen for succession.
- As history has recorded, dynasty and dynastical succession often end up with a lot of violence and physical elimination of the rivals by an aspiring person who thinks and believes that he alone is fit for succession and anyone else posing as a rival or threat should be physically eliminated. The corridors of Indian history have been splashed with the blood

of many such aspirants and their opponents (elimination of all brothers by Mughal emperor – Aurangazeb (1666 AD - 1707 AD) and Chandashoka, ruler of Magadh kingdom (299 BC -273 BC) as an illustration). In all such cases, physical usurpation of the seat of power which is the sole objective of the aspirant in question was preceded by acts of physical elimination through violence, wanton cruelty and bloodbath. Gomateswar (whose 58 feet statue is worshipped at Sravanbelgola in Hassan district of Karnataka state) who was the rightful heir to his father's throne renounced it, renounced the world, threw off his clothes out of utter disenchantment with the world and people around and retreated to the forest as there were other claimants to the throne and Gomateswar did not want any rivalry, bitterness and bloodshed arising out of the issue of succession to the throne.

- Since dynastical succession is not based on merit and is often associated with deceit and fraud, chicanery, inducement and many such undesirable practices; this is likely to wreck havoc on the well-being of subjects which should be the primary consideration for occupying the seat of power.
- Those who succeed to the seat of power (where succession is determined by lineage) most often being devoid of merit and ability themselves, stoop low to sell the good name of the person whom they succeed while indulging in vilification of their opponents. They also commit

unpardonable crimes by taking recourse to fraudulent methods for retention of power without any qualm or compunction.

The insight of Dharmapada in perceiving dynasty as something not in conformity with the law of Nature and not conducive to public good was proved correct when Indradyumna, King of Malwa prayed to Lord Jagannath that there should be no children to succeed him as having children would result in rivalry, usurpation and abuse of power and authority and would contribute to undermining all the good deeds of the past.

The French Revolution of 1789 principally rested on the guiding principle of 'worth' rather than 'birth' being the essential determining attribute or character for acquisition of power.

This is how Dharmapada had very appropriately explained to his father that in the event of his (Dharmapada's) absence he should not be unduly worried about the line of succession.

Other Characters in Dharmpada

In addition to Dharmapada, a few other characters have been introduced in this great lyric. These are Puranic and historical ones such as Jajati Keshari, Indradyumna, Anang Bhim Deva, Langula Narasimha Deva, Sadashib Samantray (Sibei Santra), Dhruba, Prahlada, Eklavya, Abhimanyu, king Sibi, sage Dadhichi and Suka muni. A brief description about all these characters has been given in the appendix.

Bishu Maharana, his wife i.e. Dharmapada's mother and the twelve hundred artisans constitute the other major characters in the lyric. A brief description about Dharmapada's mother has been given while depicting vatsalya rasa (related to filial love).

To elaborate, she was both a totally dedicated wife and a doting mother. She courageously put up with the pangs of separation from her husband for twelve long years and yet did not allow her personal anguish to overtake her duties and responsibilities as a mother in giving the best of upbringing, education and training to her son. As a matter of fact, she imparted to Dharmapada the best of scriptural, spiritual and sculptural knowledge, which is most praiseworthy, considering the fact that she came from a modest rural background without adequate exposure to education. Even against Dharmapada's tormentor, she had no malice or ill will and she condoned the lapses on his part on the ground that he was as young as her son and was not sufficiently aware of the consequences of his action and conduct. This shows how large hearted and forgiving she was. She was intensely devoted to both her husband and son. When Dharmapada finally made up his mind to leave for Chandrabhaga to meet Bishu Maharana – his father, the mother graciously permitted him to undertake the journey. Additionally, she packed the juicy berry fruits grown in the family garden and being aware of her husband's fondness for these fruits, asked Dharmapada to carry them with care. The kindness and compassion of a woman, the devotion of a wife and the care and concern of a mother for her son have been folded into one & succinctly presented by the poet through the character of Padmavati in a normal, natural and effortless manner.

Bishu Maharana, the father was the chief mason, artist and sculptor of the Sun temple at Konark who was invited by Sibei Santra, the Minister and chief architect to the king. He was the principal adviser to the chief architect about the design of the temple and how it should take the shape of a chariot yoked to seven horses driven by Lord Sun himself. His wife was four months pregnant when he left for the temple construction site. The construction of the grand temple which was 230 ft high with exquisite artistry and splendour was a long drawn-out affair, taking a heavy toll of time, energy and resources – human, material and financial. Despite frantic efforts and a lot of unceasing manual labour, the temple top could not be successfully fixed. Every time the stone was taken to be fixed on the Kalas of the temple, it came crashing down. All twelve hundred masons were exasperated and had given up hope of bringing the construction work to a logical close. The king had lost his patience and out of impatience, anxiety and anger, he had fixed a deadline of two days for sealing the temple top failing which all twelve hundred artisans were to be beheaded. It was at this critical hour of a grave crisis that Dharmapada reached the site, met his father and other artisans, heard the entire story of enormous efforts having been made and yet not succeeding to fix the temple top, the king's command about beheading of the artisans in the event of the temple top not being fixed in two days' time and ventured to take up the work. On his successful accomplishment of the mission, he was dismayed to find that a sense of fear and anxiety amounting to trepidation had gripped the mind of the artisans. Having come to know the cause of the fear, he made up his mind to sacrifice his life so that the life, dignity, and esteem of the artisans may be saved. Simultaneously, he posed a question to his father as to who was the liability he or the twelve hundred artisans. He asked his father where he stood on this.

The father was unable to weigh and balance the two and was at a loss to respond. He acknowledged the worth of the life of a bright, intelligent and exceptionally talented son like Dharmapada and was not prepared to sacrifice him. He was also not prepared to sacrifice the interests of the members of the clan either. Being placed between the two horns of a dilemma, he remained clueless, speechless, crestfallen and indecisive.

The portrayal of the character of the father Bishu Maharana, in the lyric (which is a tragedy), is perfect and could not have been better. It is but normal and natural that a father like Bishu Maharana, being placed in an extremely wearisome situation as he was, could not have been decisive and could not have given a straight, pointed and decisive reply to the son's puzzling question which on the face of it was quite disturbing. It is only at a later stage that the father comes to realise the true worth of his son and says that he does not need the twelve hundred artisans in the following words:

> The twelve hundred artisans
> Are no doubt our kith and kin
> Who have sustained our lineage
> But I do not need them (at this hour of my life).
> If, instead, I have a son
> Of your ability, merit and acumen
> The pride and esteem of my clan
> Will remain ever intact. **Verse 160**

But by then it was too late and Dharmapada's mind

having been made up (in the direction of self-sacrifice), no amount of cajoling or supplication by the father had any impact on him.

'Dharmapada' is a tragedy involving voluntary sacrifice of the life of a twelve-year-old boy who is yet to cross the threshold of childhood. This would not have been a tragedy if the father would have been firm and decisive and said, "Come what may, I am not permitting you to leave me." Looking at it from yet another angle, it may be said that it was a clear and conscious decision on the part of the poet to portray the father's character in the manner in which it has appeared in the lyric as any other treatment would have diluted the exalted character of the central hero of the lyric i.e. Dharmapada and he would not have come out in the same lofty manner as it has from the beginning till the end.

Coming to the twelve hundred artisans, they were no doubt highly skilled, having raised temples, forts, bridges, palatial mansions and innumerable objects of historical and cultural heritage, that were feasts for the eyes of mankind all over the State. If 'Utkal' literally means a land of the finest art, it is largely on account of the artistic ingenuity, creativity and skill of these artisans transmitted through successive generations which have kept it alive.

But these artisans, despite the outstanding skill possessed by them, lacked certain basic qualities of head and heart and lacked a degree of altruism, care and consideration for others. At a grave hour of crisis which was man-made and could straightaway be attributed to flawed determination of the center of gravity (on account of which the Chuda (Dadhinauti) could not be firmly and securely fixed on the Kalas of the temple), they indulged in infructuous debates through arguments and counter arguments for hours without getting at the root of the problem. Even when Dharmapada volunteered with all humility to attend to the unfinished work relating to sealing the temple top, they spoke in varying tones and were not gracious enough to accord him necessary permission in the first instance. They eventually agreed to entrust this responsibility only when they totally failed and barely a portion of one night was left before the deadline was to come to an end.

What was the basic problem or defect which the twelve hundred artisans failed to diagnose even after frantic efforts?

The top of the temple was connected to a magnet. A powerful magnet was fixed at the time of construction of 'Garvagriha' (Sanctum). There is a stone at the top and on the top of that stone there is a 'Kalas. While fixing the Chuda or Dadhinauti on the top of the 'Kalas', it did not get correctly fixed but instead, came crashing down. The fixation of 'Kalas' itself was defective. Understandably the center of gravity was not correctly determined. The center of gravity has to be exactly in the center of the top of the temple and the consequence of the slightest deviation in correctly determining the center would be disastrous.

Once Dharmapada with his uncanny intelligence and piercing insight derived from a study of the 'Shilpa Shastra' in childhood under the able guidance of his mother, succeeded in diagnosing this major defect, there was no difficulty to refix the 'Kalas' and the Chuda or Dadhinauti on the 'Kalas'. This is how the temple top was sealed and the work of construction of the temple going on for twelve long years came to a logical close in the shortest possible time.

There is a saying in English that the greatest strength of a man or woman's character lies in acknowledging his/her own mistake(s).

In this case, tragically enough, even after the defect was diagnosed by Dharmapada, the artisans who had been struggling hard to fix the Chuda on the 'Kalas' did not graciously acknowledge their own ignorance or their failure to solve a structural problem which was their own creation. (The lyric 'Dharmapada' does not indicate as such). Initially, after Dharmapada completed the unfinished task and the temple top was sealed, the artisans were lost in boisterous acclamation and jubilation. The initial fervour, however, did not last long but was replaced by inexplicable envy, exaggerated sense of self-importance and excessive survival instinct. It is this survival instinct which made the artisans seethe with an unfounded apprehension which manifested itself in an unexpected and totally avoidable spirit of disaffection against Dharmapada.

The artisans could have been discrete and gracious enough not to openly express their dismay amounting to envy against Dharmapada being honoured in the royal court by the king being fully aware of the fact that (a) they were Dharmapada's father's age (b) they were far more experienced than Dharmapada (c) both their age and experience should have made them kinder, nobler, more mature and gracious (d) no father would ever openly express such envy against the son (e) the vast difference in age should have prompted them to soften their stand, made them large hearted and they should have demonstrated affection, tolerance and much more patience, resilience and restraint, as also respect for the incredible and uncommon acumen and skill displayed by Dharmapada and (f) getting beheaded was an unfounded fear in as much as the same was related to the contingency of non-completion of the temple which did not exist after the temple top was sealed by Dharmapada. When the fear is irrational and exaggerated, it amounts to phobia in the phraseology of psychiatry or the science of mental health. The twelve hundred artisans by their strange attitude, action and unpardonable conduct had unfortunately dragged themselves to such a pathetic situation.

Langula Narasimha Dev, son of king Ananga Bhim Deva 3 and queen Kasturi Debi, ruled Odisha (then Utkal) from 1239 AD to 1264 AD. He was a great warrior, had conquered what was then known as Bengal, annexed Midnapore, Hooghly and Howrah districts to Utkal, had fought fiercely the sea pirates at Tamralipta port (which is now in West Bengal State), fully conquered and repulsed them and in the process of registering one victory after another in the east, north and south against his adversaries, had acquired vast fortunes. The treasury of the kingdom was full (this is evident from the fact that the king had no hesitation to spend 17.5 lakh tolas of gold in construction of the Konark temple which at the relevant point of time would be equivalent to Rupees 40 crore). He had got a huge fortress constructed at Raibania in Balasore to protect the sovereignty of the State from foreign invasion. He was a lover of art, literature and culture. He patronised construction of a large number of temples with the Sun temple at Konark climaxing the highest form of artistic and sculptural beauty and excellence. This temple had engaged him, his minister and chief architect Shri Shibei Santra and twelve hundred masons/artisans/sculptors for twelve long years (1239-1250) in addition to enormous resources being spent from the State exchequer.

India's most celebrated poet Kalidas in his most illustrious work *Abhijnanamsakuntalam* has, in the following three beautiful verses, vividly described the role and responsibility of a king, how burdensome is the seat of power and how a king, who has the welfare of his subjects as the primary concern of his heart, should conduct himself:

Sanskrit

Ausukyamatra nabasadayati pratistha
Klisnati labdha paripalana bruttireba
Natishramapaynaya yatha shramay
Rajyam swahasta dhrutadanda
mibatapatram.

English translation

Supreme power merely relieves fervent
longing. The very task of protecting what is
obtained is burdensome. Thus, a kingdom
like an umbrella, the handle of which is
held in one's own hand is not so much for
removal of fatigue as for fatigue (itself).

Canto 5, Verse 6, *Abhijnanamsakuntalam*

II

Sanskrit

Swasukhanirabhilasa khidyate lokaheto
Pratidinamaya ba te bruttirebam bidhaiba
Anubhabati hi murdhna padapa teebram
usnam
Shramayati pantam chayaya sansritanam

English translation

Regardless of personal comfort, you daily toil for the good of the subjects (under you) or, such indeed is your daily course of action. For the tree suffering burning heat on its head, allays by its shade, the pain of those who take shelter under it.

Canto 5, Verse 7, ***Abhijnanamsakuntalam***

III

Sanskrit

Niyamayasi bimarga prasthitanattadandah
Prasamayasi bibadam kalpase rakshanaya
Atanusu bibhabesu gyatayah santu nama
Twayi tu parisamaptam bandhukrutyam
prajanam

English translation

With the royal staff (in your hand), you restrain those that follow the wrong path: you put down disputes and are competent

> to protect your people. Wealth being
> plentiful, one may have indeed, a number
> of relations but in you are consummated the
> duties of kinsmen of the subjects.
> **Canto 5, Verse 8,** *Abhijnanamsakuntalam*

Judged by these standards, Langula Narasimha Deva was no doubt an illustrious ruler. In terms of extraordinary physical prowess and military genius and skills, he was second to none. Whether it was Kashmir or Bengal or Gouda or Raada or Lucknowti or Deccan he ruthlessly suppressed all kingdoms which posed a threat to his supremacy. He was also an ardent lover of art, literature and culture.

The supremacy of a ruler does not, however, lie alone in his success in battles waged against adversaries. It lies in maintaining a perfect balance in day-to-day action and personal conduct (as opposed to extremes) which should be actuated by altruism, moderation and restraint on one hand and acting as an instrument of even handed and fair justice to one and all (friends and foes alike) on the other. It also simultaneously lies in being kind and compassionate to the subjects (without compromising discipline), protecting the weak & helpless and making unceasing efforts for their total well-being.

While king Langula Narasimha Dev was clearly conscious of his obligations towards protection of the suzerainty of his kingdom and unmitigated welfare of his subjects, he was obsessed with achieving something great and magnificent like construction of the Sun temple at Konark which would be unparalleled in terms of its artistic grandeur and finesse.

As Dr Sigmund Freud, one of the most distinguished psychologists of the twentieth century (1856-1939) had said, "Everything you and I do springs from two motives i.e. the sexual urge and the desire to be great. The desire to be great means the desire to be important."

Viewed in that sense, there was prima facie nothing wrong on the part of king Langula Narasimha Deva to patronise construction of a world-renowned temple at Konark. As a matter of fact, in its visualisation, planning and design, it was extraordinary. It involved a time span of twelve long years, mobilisation of twelve hundred artisans from all parts of the State and ensured their continued presence at the worksite, making them bereft of any contact with the families left behind or any other human/social relations.

The desire, however, to be great or important can be achieved either by demonstrating proven physical prowess or by knowledge and intellect of a razor-sharp mind through which one's opponents or detractors could be brought around (like Jagadguru Adi Shankaracharya did in 8th century AD) but certainly not by promoting a culture of unquestioned obedience or acquiescence which could work havoc as it did in case of king Langula Narasimha Deva.

The culture of acquiescence is the single biggest drawback in monarchy (or dictatorship), in which whatever is desired or directed or decreed by the king becomes the last word, almost like the law of the land and none else can afford to disagree or disobey or transgress in terms of its compliance except with the disastrous consequence of meeting a severe reprisal by way of punishment going up to death penalty. In such a scenario, there is no scope for any tolerance for dissent as any and every such dissent is sought to be ruthlessly suppressed.

A gigantic work of raising a superstructure like the Sun temple at Konark with specimens of such artistic beauty and finesse cannot be carried to its logical conclusion in haste and inadvertence. Regretfully, as the legend goes, not only the duration of completion was reduced at the final stage of construction of the temple from four to two months (with a view to have the ceremony related to the completion of the temple (Mandir pratistha and puja) on the seventh day of the bright lunar fortnight in the month of Magha (January) but a deadline of two days was fixed to seal the temple top failing which the twelve hundred artisans were to be beheaded.

This was an act of indiscretion combined with wanton cruelty. It is anathema to modern civilised human conscience. It is the negation of inalienable human right to life (Art 21 of the Constitution). It is antipodal to human dignity and decency which is the very quintessence of human right. It may be appropriate to quote the following verse from mahakavya 'Kiratarjuniam' by the noted Sanskrit poet Bharavi:

> **Sanskrit**
>
> Sahasa bidadheeta na kriyam
> Abibeka paramapadam padam
> Brunate hi bimrusyakarinam
> Gunalubdha swayameba sampada.
>
> **English translation**
>
> One should not do anything in haste or
> with an element of indiscretion. Want of
> due discretion and deliberation is a sure
> source of calamities. Fortunes that are
> ever attached to merits, seek of their own
> motion, one who acts with circumspection
> (proper thought).
>
> **Canto 2, Verse 30,** *Kiratarjuniyam*

Such a command worked havoc. It set in motion a lot of negative trends. It adversely affected the psyche of the artisans. It completely demoralised and demotivated them. The freedom and spontaneity of human spirit was shattered beyond restoration.

That the Chuda was not getting fixed on top of the temple despite unceasing efforts and that the completion of the temple was getting inordinately delayed may have led the king to impatience, restlessness, anger and frustration. That, however, should not have gone to the extent of provoking him to issue a command that the twelve hundred artisans will be beheaded if the feat is not accomplished in two days, which considering the total duration of construction of the temple, the very size, its majesty combined with artistry and finesse was too short a time span.

In issuing the command, the king lost sight of the fact that twelve hundred artisans having left their hearth and home had unremittingly engaged themselves for twelve long years, forgetting all their creature comforts, leisure as also time for their food, sleep and rest. Some of them had died in the process of such an excruciatingly painful engagement for such a long period in the extreme heat of the sun. Dr Kartikeawar Patra, eminent historian and researcher has brought out the immensity of this human tragedy in his much-acclaimed work, 'Katha kahe Konark' or 'Konark speaks' and I reproduce below the English translation of the pathetic and heart-rending reaction of the family members (including women and children) of the twelve hundred artisans on the uncertainty of the homecoming of the latter:

"No doubt, the Maharaja is constructing a grand temple but our plight and predicament baffle description. Years have rolled by but he (the head of the family) is yet to return. We are passing our days in great distress. How long will the construction of the temple take? When will my master return? Is the king ever perturbed that by detaining my master (in the said construction work) he has made us rot in utter misery and suffering? A sickly child is lamenting before his mother thus: O, my mother! when will my father return? O, king! please return my father to me as without him I will not live long."

One is reminded of the English saying, "Power corrupts and absolute power corrupts absolutely." The king in this case was no doubt holding the reins of absolute power but that should not have blinded him to issue such an inappropriate, indiscrete and unjust order which was also cruel and heartless, to say the least. The cannons of propriety and fairness warranted that the king should have directed Shri Sibei Santra, his minister and chief architect to investigate into the cause of the Chuda or Dadhinauti not being able to be fixed on top of the Kalas of the temple in an appropriate manner within a stipulated time.

One is also reminded of yet another saying in English such as, "Some are born great, some achieve greatness while greatness is thrust on a few." In this case, the king no doubt inherited greatness from his father Ananga Bhim Deva 3 but he was himself was obsessed with greatness such as great kingdoms, unrivalled supremacy in power and authority, great temples, great works of art, architecture and sculpture and great workmanship. Such an obsession could sometimes be lethal. Without issue of such an order, the precious life of a precocious divine child representing the best of innocence, best of humility, best of humanism and rarest of the rare creative talent and professional excellence for that incredibly young age would not have withered away.

A realisation should have dawned spontaneously on the sense and conscience of the king that (a) lives of twelve hundred artisans once taken away (by the cruel act of beheading) cannot be restored to them and their families (b) such mass killing is too gruesome to be imagined (c) a void would be caused by the death of twelve hundred artisans which will not be able to be filled (d) this would cause a colossal loss to the kingdom in as much as the skills acquired by the artisans over years cannot be transmitted across generations; it is a loss forever.

The poet Gopabandhu has written in the concluding lines of Dharmapada:

'Neither Dharmapada is there nor the temple. It is only the legend which lives.'

In a similar vein, one can say that neither the king nor the chief architect nor the artisans, nor the king's obsession to be great and to create objects of superb workmanship has survived. They all have been consumed by the 'Maha Kala' or the supreme devourer.

To conclude on a sad and poignant note, whether it is the Sun temple at Konark or the majestic Vishnu temple at Siem Rip, Cambodia or the most beautiful monuments at Borobudur (Buddhist stupas) in Indonesia or the massive Shwe Dagon Pagoda of Myanmar or the Leaning Tower of Pisa, Italy or the old city of Jerusalem or Hanging Gardens of Babylon, or the Great Pyramid of Giza, Egypt or Lighthouse of Alexandriya or the Great wall of China or the Colossus of Rhodes or the Statue of Zeus at Olympia in Greece or countless forms of intricate design and sheer beauty of workmanship elsewhere which till date continue to be feasts for the eyes of mankind, could not have been erected without years of hard, unceasing and backbreaking manual labour by numerous masons, artisans, sculptors and architects. Some or many of these structures might have withered away on the sands of time while a few might have remained with bruises all over their bodies. These structures would have involved transportation of heavy materials (stones, pillars, logs of wood) from far-off distances (like black granite stone from Nilgiri sub-division of Balasore for the Sun temple at Konark, stones from the Blue Mountains of Cambodia for the historic temple structures at Siem Rip). They would have involved equally strenuous efforts to lift such heavy objects atop the temple/pagoda/stupa. The efforts to chisel, level and polish the stones so that life can be infused in the inanimate and the stones can speak, smile, dance, sing, play musical instruments and cry in anguish would have been equally extraordinary.

The few objects of beauty, majesty and finesse which remain intact or even bruised are silent witnesses of and eloquent testimonies to the blood, sweat, tears, toil and travail of numerous masons, artisans and sculptors. There would have been many Bishu Maharanas and Dharmapadas who would have poured their uncanny imagination, ingenuity, creativity and artistic skill to make the inanimate and voiceless stones speak.

It may not be out of place to state that the Sun temple at Konark is not only unmatched in terms of finesse of a grand design and exquisite artistic and sculptural majesty and beauty but has also inspired a generation of poets, painters and playwrights to give vent to their romantic passion and creativity in the shape of priceless art. Of them, in particular, I would like to share with the readers flashes of such art from the poetic creation of two celebrities namely Pandit Neelakantha Dash (1884-1967) and Shri Sachi Routray (1913-2004).

The first has a romantic background which I would like to share with the readers. In October 1917, Pandit Neelakantha Dash who was then the Vice-Chancellor of Satyabadi Vidyapeeth (founded by Pandit Gopabandhu Dash) had been on a visit to the Konark temple on the Kumar Purnima day, a day of festivities in Odisha which comes four days after Vijaya Dashami. Their journey was disrupted by gusts of wind and heavy rain. The teacher and the students took shelter in Ramchandi temple which is located on a heap of sand at the mouth of river Kushabhadra and about 5-kms south-west of the Konark temple. The students slept inside the temple but the teacher could not.

He was wide awake throughout the night. The reminiscences of a hoary past, those of the Kalinga empire which at one point of time in history expanded from river Ganges in the north to river Kaberi in the south, with finest specimens of excellence in art, literature and sculpture which justified the name 'Utkal', the hoary tradition of naval trade undertaken by the 'sadhabas' (trader navigators) of Utkal in faraway lands of Java, Sumatra, Borneo and Bali (of the present day Indonesia), how bouts of foreign invasion brought devastation to this land of bounty, beauty and majesty and reduced the State to its present level of poverty flashed across the poet's mind.

This is how 'Konarke,' an outpouring of a troubled but intensely sensitive heart was born. Without delving deep into the contents of this magnum opus of an eminent poet, teacher, historian, freedom fighter and legislator, I would like to share with the readers 10 stanzas translated by me from the original 'Konarke' in Oriya to English (stanzas 740 to 750) through which the poet has given vent to his nostalgic and inquisitive thoughts about Konark temple, that magnificent specimen of artistic beauty and splendour:

On this land
Who built such fabulous objects
Which are at once
Manifestations of such majesty, beauty and grace
Who dug up the heart of the river (Chandrabhaga)
And filled it with so many stones
With such courage, intelligence and skill
How many mountains of lofty heights were cut?
How were such huge pieces of stones transported
To a distant landscape with vast stretches of sand?
Tell me to remove doubts from my mind
How the soft and gentle breeze
Could pierce through such large but cute bodies
Which have been carved out of stones?
How were stones of such large size
Lifted atop the temple of such height with such ease?
What were the equipments used (when there were no cranes)?
With what fertile imagination and dexterity
The proud artisans of Utkal could carve out
Objects of such majesty and beauty?
How could life be infused
Into a mass of lifeless stones?
Years have rolled by
These objects of beauty
Have no doubt been hard hit
By the (saline)blow of the wind

Coming from the sea;
They look nevertheless
As perennially fresh as life itself
And produce a feeling
On the onlooker's mind
As if they have been produced
Only the day before.

Shri Sachidananda Routray, yet another noted poet of Odisha has, in his anthology of poems called 'Pandulipi' (1947) while expressing the excitement, wonder and joy as also the sadness of his heart after looking at those marvellous objects of majesty and beauty, has poured out his gratitude to countless un-named masons, artisans and sculptors for their 'blood, sweat and tears' through which they could create such priceless objects which continue to be the feasts for the eyes of mankind. I quote from a few stanzas of that heart-rending anthology:

You have seen
The manifestation of a bewitching art
Which brings life to inanimate rocks
But I have seen instead
A mount of million bones of broken hearts.

You have seen
How poetry has manifested itself
In the lifeless body of stones

How dreams of drowsiness
Have drowned themselves
In bottomless depths of immortal love.

I have retreated from the lion's gate
Poor, pitiable and unromantic
With accumulated anguish of a heavy heart
I have looked at the temple's incomparable beauty.

With the eyes of a craftsman
With the lamp of my agony
I offer my obeisance to the masons and artisans
Who through their, 'blood, sweat and tears'
Have crafted and infused life, beauty and romance
Into multiple lifeless objects.

I have seen so many masons and craftsmen
Have buried themselves in the grave of art,
How they have suffered endless agonies,
How their backbones have been crushed and severed
By the sheer weight of stones
Which they have carried like animals on their head.

I salute you
O, masons and craftsmen,
I salute the majesty and versatility of your genius;
You have transmitted a unique message

Into millions of hearts,
You have departed to your grave on the sands of time
Singing the glory of the king
Being totally oblivious of anything in return.

The best way of offering our silent tribute to Dharmapada's extraordinary genius as well as homage for the sacrifice he most unreservedly made to save the life, dignity and self-esteem of others would be to remember and translate to action in our daily lives what he had advocated before Bishu Maharana, his father and conclude:

One may get destroyed
But many may unfold
And elevate themselves,
One diminishes
Many arise and uphold,
In one person's decline and decay
Lies the evolution of many.

DHARMAPADA

A TRIBUTE TO THE ODIA LEGEND

After offering prayers to the creator who is immanent, all pervasive, all-encompassing and infinitely merciful and also to river Chandrabhaga, Dharmapada jumps from the temple top to the river and the sea down below and sacrifices his life for the cause of holding the safety, security, dignity and esteem of the life of 1200 artisans.

Twelve-year-old boy Dharmapada
Bright, intelligent and innocent,
Has neither heard nor known
About his father ever from anyone. (1)

Right from birth
He has been happily nurtured by his mother,
Overwhelmed with her tender love and care;
Himself deeply kind and compassionate
Cannot think of hurting even a fly or insect. (2)

It is twelve years since
Dharmapada's father left home;
The mother has endured
The pangs of separation
in her stride
By looking at the son's face
She cannot stand
Even a speck of dust falling on him. (3)

Right from his childhood
She makes him learn with care
Nuances of the ancestral lore;
With his sharp memory
He assimilates and retains
Whatever he listens, observes and learns
Remains imprinted in his receptive mind. (4)

Being a playful child
He plays with the children of his age,
On the dust of the village soil
He creates and recreates
Temples, artefacts and mansions,
Brilliant are his insight and creative skills. (5)

Those around him
Who look at the specimens of his art
Are struck by his dexterity and skill
And exclaim, "If he lives long
he will surely distinguish himself as one
In a countless number, unmatched". (6)

Dharmapada is keen and eager
To know and learn
The science of masonry and sculpture.
His mother has instilled in him thus
"If you read
You will know, O, my loved one!
If you know
You will triumph."
We have, she says,
"The treasure store
Of knowledge (of all arts)
Deeply embedded
In your (much cherished) ancestral lore." (7)

Enrolled in the village school
At the tender age of five;
He being bright and intelligent
Acquired mastery in a short time,
Whatever was taught and learnt. (8)

He learnt and acquired mastery
Over a variety of scriptures;
The characters and mythological events
Depicted in (Bhagabat) Geeta, Bhagabat and other Puranas
From construction of temples to digging of tanks,
He demonstrated his uncanny skills
Over whatever he read, learnt and practised. (9)

By temperament
He was affectionate and considerate,
Had malice towards none.
He always looked upon himself
As one amongst many
And never erected a wall of division
Between him and his companions.
The same, however, was
Not true of a few mates
Who were envious of him
While caring for others. (10)

Away from the class
He studied at home
And learnt how to be an artisan
With focused attention.
He learnt how to carve
Images out of wood and stone
Of temples, chariots and palaces
By infusing life in the lifeless. (11)

One day he returned from school
And stood before his mother
With tearful eyes and a pale face
He was sad and speechless. (12)

The mother most anxious to know
The source of his depression and gloom,
She quickly enquires of him
Why does he look so dejected
Why is there no laughter in his face? (13)

She sadly recalls the old days
When Dharmapada back from school
Would share with much jubilation
So many lively episodes of life,
Seeing his face bereft of smile
She was struck with fear and pain. (14)

She enquired of him
"Has your teacher punished (you)?
Has any of your mates scolded (you?
Who has caused such loss of dignity and why
At the school or anywhere outside." (15)

"By your sweet temperament
And dignified conduct
You have rightly earned
The love and good will of all.
Share with me
And remove my doubts
By unfolding whatever has happened
At the school or anywhere outside." (16)

"If there are tears in your eyes
O, my dear child!
If you do not unfold
What has happened,
Don't you know
That seeing your condition
I would be struck by thunder
And would fall down
As good as dead"? (17)

"Don't you know
That I have got you

O, the darling of my heart!
After worshipping
So many Gods and Goddesses?
I am a poor woman
And you are my dearest object,
The sheet-anchor of my being
I am ready to die a thousand deaths
So that you may live with dignity and grace. (18)

I have spent this desolate life
So long and so far
Only by looking at your lovely face.
O, the moon of my clan!
You are like a garland around
The neck of a begging woman,
Please share with me
Whatever has happened
And whatever thought is bothering you. (19)

Soothed by his mother's words
Dharmapada forgot for a moment
The source and cause of his torment
And asked O, my mother!
Please tell me if we have a clan
And, if so, who is my father
(Is he alive or dead
And if alive, is he near or far)? (20)

The mother failed to comprehend
And asked Dharmapada
What made you ask?
On return from your class
Such probing questions
With such restlessness
Which you had
Never before asked. (21)

The son unfolds,
Today something happened in the classroom
Something (highly objectionable) was told
By a classmate to me
Which filled me with agony and shame,
Which continues to torment me
And I am unable to lift my head. (22)

I was at school
Attending to my lessons (as usual)
When the lead pencil
Slipped out of my hand.
I requested the boy
Who was sitting next to me
O, brother! would you be nice
To collect the lead pencil
And give it back to me? (23)

He not only refused
But ridiculed me instead
And called me (most inappropriately) 'Ababua',[1]
He further said most disrespectfully
"How dare you address me as your brother
And issue a command
To denigrate me in the eyes of others? (24)

Other classmates initially kept cool
But burst out later with a quiet laughter;
Silently and with my head
Bent low with shame
I collected the lead pencil
And quietly took my seat thereafter. (25)

Tell me O, my mother!
Without fear and shame
Touch my body and speak
What is our clan?
Who is my father?
Where is he?
That will remove from my mind
All my doubts, confusion and pain. (26)

---

1 'Ababua' in English means a fatherless child. It could also mean a 'bastard' whose father is not known.

Seething with rage
The mother burst out
In an uproarious voice,
Who is that imbecile scum
Who could thus insult my son
Without any rhyme or reason?
Is his mother so chaste
That he dares address
My son as 'Ababua' or fatherless? (27)

The mother soon thereafter
Softened her tone and temper
And said, "After all he is also a child
As tender as Dharmapada,
Who (because of his age)
Is not sufficiently aware
Of the consequences
Of what he says and does,
Of what use, therefore,
Is it to show 'tooth for tooth'
Or 'eye for eye'?"
It will not take me anywhere. (28)

The mother proceeded further,
"I do not know
But have heard in my young days
From people of older generations.

Your father, grandfather and great grandfather
Have all been sculptors, masons and artisans
Of valour and fame for posterity;
Please understand this without any difficulty." (29)

They all owe
Their illustrious origin to Lord Viswakarma,
The divine 'builder'
And decidedly the best
Among all other artistes.
They have left their footprints
On the sands of time
The marvels of their imperishable fame. (30)

She continued further,
"Indradyumna, (the king of Malwa)
Invited artisans and sculptors
From various parts of the country;
Mobilised and harnessed their talent and skill
To construct the temple of
Lord Shri Jagannath at Puri. (31)

They were the salt of the earth
Of tested and proven worth,
And were all honoured
By the king,
Who tied 'sarees' to their heads

(As was the prevalent custom then)
And the temple at the sacred Nilachal Dham
Was put in place. (32)

Years later, she continued,
"The said temple was renovated
By your forefathers
With the patronage of king Jajati
(Of the famed 'Soma' dynasty).
They had all lived up to
The king's expectations
And thus preserved
The reputation and glory of the clan." (33)

Years later, she further continued
(In the middle of the twelfth century),
The temple was reconstructed
By king Ananga Bhim Deva 2 of Chola dynasty.
The said temple has till date survived
The onslaughts of time
Like a pillar of imperishable fame,
Of beauty, finesse and grace. (34)

The artistry, creativity and skill
Of your illustrious forefathers
Lie hidden in the stones and statues
Of these temples.

They stand
As silent but grand witnesses
Of your clan's glory and excellence. (35)

She continued further,
"When King Kharavela
In the evening of his life
(At the height of his glory)
Resolved to renounce the world
And spend his last days
Like an ascetic inside a cave
Along with his consort(s),
And lead a quiet life
Amidst other ascetics,
It is only your forefathers
Who constructed those caves
At Khandagiri (Bhubaneswar)
Known as 'Ranihansapura".
Even today,
More than two thousand years after,
Those caves have remained
As silent witnesses
Of that exotic artistry and grace. (36)

In the eleventh century,
She further continued,
"On the bank of river Baitarani

Jajati Keshari, (the king of 'Soma' dynasty)
Organised a huge sacrificial fire
(called Dashaswamedha Yagya)
for which, as the legend goes,
The Gods and Goddesses
Came down from heaven to participate.
The rhythmic force
With which the four Vedas were recited
Reverberated
Through the waves of the river (Baitarani)
Across the hills, dales, streams,
Mountains and forests of the State. (37)

From the said sacrificial fire
Had emerged Goddess 'Biraja',
The 'transcendental' and 'effulgent',
Whose lustre had spread
Across the length and breadth of the land. (38)

Your forefathers once again
Constructed the temple (at Jajpur),
Dedicated to 'Biraja' Goddess,
Where idols of seven mothers
(Sapta Matrukas: please see at the end of the appendix)
And holy pillars stand installed.
Do not have the slightest doubt

O, my son!
That you are the progeny of those
Illustrious artisans and sculptors. (39)

In Ekamra Kanan,
(which is the present-day city of Bhubaneswar)
(The city of over three hundred temples),
It was your forefathers once again
Who raised those matchless structures
One more artistic and beautiful than the other.
With Lord Shiva as their presiding deity
On whose forehead shines the moon;
Do not have the slightest doubt
That their blood
Flows through your arteries and veins,
You are the progeny
Of those illustrious artisans. (40)

She continued further,
"My father-in-law (Dharmapada's grandfather)
Went to Cuttack
For renovation of Barabati Fort,
He did not return
But was detained (by the king)
As the work was incomplete
And there without any care
He died a painful death.

On hearing the sad news of his tragic end
My mother-in-law (your grandmother)
Lost consciousness
And eventually died of shock." (41)

The mother said further,
"Since the day your father left home
And departed for a distant land
I have been haunted
Day-in and day-out
By his sweet memories
As also by the pangs of separation.
For long twelve years
Passage of just a day for me
Sounds like the end of a millennium!
Day-after-day
Month-after-month
I pine for his company
And wistfully long his return,
I am drained of blood
And unable to breathe." (42)

She continued further,
"If I am alive today
It is because of you
Who is with me in flesh and blood.
Separation from your father

Bishu Maharana who has been selected by Sadashiva Samantray, Chief Architect and Minister to king Langula Narasimha Dev-I, as the chief architect and adviser is proceeding to Konark, the venue of the temple, leaving his wife – Padmavati who was in the family way behind.

Makes me feel benumbed,
But when I look at your face
I muster the will to live
For, you are
The very apple of my eyes. (43)

Thus spoke Dharmapada's mother,
Overwhelmed with emotion
Stung by intense agony and pain.
She cast her face down
And started weeping,

Tears incessantly trickled down
Her cheeks. (44)

Sitting in the lap of his mother
Dharmapada asked
Struck with fear and dismay,
"Why are you O, my mother!
In such stressful tears?"
He went on consoling her,
Wiping out the tears
With the help
Of the border of her garment. (45)

Dharmapada asked
"Where is my father?
Since when did he leave home?
For what purpose?
Where is he (now)
And how far is the place
Where he is at work?
How long will it take
For me to traverse that track?
Would I not be able to do it? (46)

He further asked,
"Don't you receive any message from him
About his health and well being?

Guide me O, mother!
As to how
I should negotiate the track
And reach the destination with ease.
I assure you, O, mother!
That if I go and reach the destination,
I must be able to find him
And bring news about his wellness
Much to your relief
Without any loss of time." (47)

The mother felt assuaged
By the assurance of the son.
In soft and sweet words
She kissed him
And breathed a sigh of relief
Out of intense emotional delight
And said, "O, my darling!
I know the agony of my suffering
Is too much for you to put up with.
When you wipe out my tears
With all the tenderness of your heart,
I feel the warmth of filial bond,
I feel assured and re-assured
Which has sustained me
For long twelve years." (48)

She continued further,
"A temple is being raised
Dedicated to Lord Sun
On the bank of the river Chandrabhaga,
At its mouth
Which is proximate to the sea-shore. (49)

King Narasimha Deva of Chola dynasty,
Under whose patronage
The temple is being built
Says with a lot of pride,
"The Sun temple will be unmatched
In its artistry and grandeur."
Your father
Is one of the twelve hundred masons/sculptors,
Who belongs to the clan of Lord Vishwakarma
And who have been selected as the very best
And invited for this purpose
By Sadasiva Samantray (Sibei Santra)
The Minister and Chief Architect to the king.
You were only four months old in my womb
When your father left.
You were born six months after
He has not returned since that date." (50)

The mother continued,
"The temple under construction

Will rest on a chariot of Lord Sun,
The God of righteousness
Who will himself drive the chariot
(With the help of seven horses).[2]
It will act as a fortress of the east
It will protect the ocean track
From invasion by the enemies (of the State)." (51)

"Since your father is working,
She continued,
For construction of a temple
Dedicated to Lord Sun
Who is the God of righteousness,
I remembered him
And named you 'Dharmapada'
With a lot of motherly love and piety." (52)

"I have not seen,
The mother continued
But have only heard
A popular adage
Which reads like this:
"A traveller may go
To river Ganges seven times

---

2 The seven horses are: Gayatri, Usmika, Anustap, Brihati, Puncti, Tristup and Jagati

But one single trip to Chandrabhaga,
The site of construction of the Sun temple
Will make his/her face
Turn pale and colourless." (53)

The mother continued further,
"Twelve years have rolled by
I have not received any news.
Day-in and day-out
I pine for him,
I worship the Gods and Goddesses of our sect
Praying for his health and well-being." (54)

"I have been meticulous
She continued,
In observance of all religious ceremonies
which includes the ritual on every Sunday.
I burn the candle round the clock
And worship the village deity.
I have virtually surrendered myself
In body, mind and spirits
To the refuge of the God of righteousness
Only to pray for his health and wellness." (55)

Dharmapada came up with a resolve
And said,
"I shall go to Chandrabhaga

Come what may,
I shall meet my father
I shall bring back with me
His hand-written letter
Carrying news about
His health and well-being." (56)

The mother reacted thus,
"O, the pupil of my eye!
How can I live
Even for a moment
Being separated from you?
You are the only light in our home
Amidst the enveloping gloom,
You are also like the key
To the treasure of my heart." (57)

She said further,
"You are the oar
With which I row the raft of my life,
You are like a supporting stick
For a person who has been
Blinded by your love.
Without you
I won't survive even for a moment
But, instead, would be drowned
In an ocean of grief." (58)

Dharmapada said,
"O, my mother!
Please permit me to leave
Of your own accord
With happiness and joy;
I must go and meet my father,
I shall no doubt return
With news about his well being
Before the expiry of the month." (59)

He further continued,
"Together with my father
I shall meet
And have a discourse
With hundreds of artisans, masons and sculptors
Who belong to our illustrious clan;
I would also see
How the chariot of Lord Sun
Is being yoked to the horses
And how the main temple
Resting on the chariot
Is being built
And carried to its logical close." (60)

He further said,
"I shall take a dip
In the holy river

And shall see Lord Sun
Emerging from the east
(Like a ball of fire
In all his redness and lustre
And the rays being diffused all over).
Please tell me without fear
How shall I
Introduce myself to my father?" (61)

The mother responded,
"O, dear!
When you have made up your mind
I would be the last person
To prevent you,
Since such prevention
Will cause you a lot of pain. (62)

She continued,
"Your father will only be
Too delighted to meet you;
You too would gain confidence
After meeting him.
You would also see
The skill of our artisans
Which in this world is unmatched.
Even though young in age
You are endowed with a fine intellect

And sharp presence of mind.
I have nothing more to add
You may do
Whatever you think is right." (63)

The mother having thus said,
Wrote down the name[3]
Of Dharmapada's father on the ground
And said,
"Recognition by your father
Will be instant;
The moment you have landed
On that soil
Where he is at work,
You have fully taken after your father
One body is a replica of the other.
(It seems as if)
A print has been taken from a mould
Making the resemblance manifold
In the eyes, nose, face and forehead
Like the sixteen digits of the moon."[4] (64)

---

3 According to a time honoured custom and tradition, women, particularly in rural Odisha, whose husbands are alive, do not utter their names but write them down either on the ground or on a piece of paper, if they are literate or take the help of the neighbour to write it down, if they are unlettered.

4 'Shola Kala' or the sixteen digits of the moon are: amrit, manada, pusa, tusti, pusti, rati, dhruti, shashi, chandrika, kanti, jyotsna, shree, preeti, angada, poorna, poornamruta

She further said,
"When the four eyes will meet
After your arrival
The two hearts will also unite.
You belong to him
He is much sought after by you,
He will be keen and eager
To embrace you
And to take you to his fold. (65)

The mother said again,
"I am still hesitant
To permit you to go alone,
Such a long distance
(Which is not straight)
Which will cause you much pain." (66)

Dharmapada said,
"Do not be afraid, O, mother!
I will be accompanied
By Balia, our old faithful pet.
Balia may have difficulty to spot
But (he) will be
Instantly spotted (by father),
Once that happens
I shall disclose to father
Full details of our home, village and my birth. (67)

The mother said,
"O, my darling!
The most precious object of my love,
You are a superb specimen
Of courage, intelligence and wit.
With the grace of Lord Jagannath
You will maintain intact
The reputation and fame
Of the illustrious members of your clan."(68)

2.

On the thirteenth day in the lunar calendar
Which the mother chose
As auspicious for the son's journey;
She worshipped the local deity Jagulei
And tied the flower
Which was offered to the deity
In a corner of the cloth
Worn by her son. (69)

She also took care
To tie in the double bagged knapsack,[5]
Put across the shoulder of her son
A few juicy berry fruits[6]

---

5 'Jaunli' is a double bagged knapsack which is carried across the shoulder of a traveller.

6 Bara Koli is a juicy fruit (berry) grown in jujube tree.

Dharmapada taking leave of his mother for his journey to Konark, after assuring her that he would be back soon with tidings about his father

Which were grown in the home garden
Which Bishu Maharana (her husband) was fond of.
She asked Dharmapada
To carry them with great care. (70)

She further said,
"This (the juicy berry fruit) will be yet another
Specimen of identity of the son
Being confirmed by the father." (71)

She invoked the blessings of Gods
Lakshmi Narasimha and Durga Madhab
To make the journey
Of her son safe and secure. (72)

Thus commenced the journey
By Dharmapada, the brave,
With blessings of his mother assured.
He proceeded towards the east
Followed by Balia, the domestic pet. (73)

He crossed countless paddy fields,
Sweet smelling grass, marshy lands and swamps;
The rivers, forests, mountains and lakes,
The intractable path in wilderness
(Strewn with thorns and thistles)
But Dharmapada, the brave was without fear;
He continued his journey day and night. (74)

He chased the sea crabs
With Balia running
In full force behind,
Being full of zest and joy.
(As he was going to meet his father)
He inscribed his name
On the traveller's path
To state that he was a pilgrim.

Dharmapada is proceeding on his journey to Konark with family pet dog Balia following close by.

Dharmapada by name
Bound on a long sojourn
To the holy Chandrabhaga
As his most cherished destination. (75)

Dharmapada kept on enquiring
(About)the correct path leading
To his destination.

The journey finally came to an end
When he arrived at the cherished land
And found twelve hundred artisans
At unceasing work, day and night
Not a moment to stand or behold. (76)

The workplace was crowded
And resounded
With a deafening noise
Where it was difficult
To distinguish day and night;
All the artisans had set
Themselves in body, mind and spirits,
No time for food and sleep
And rest even for a moment. (77)

3.

Twelve-year-old Dharmapada,
A complete stranger to the place,
He searches around
Looks in all directions,
Gazes at streams of people
Being unable to find his father.
He is worried and dumbfounded;
The strain of travel, search and wait
Clearly visible in his innocent face. (78)

Whom should I ask?
Who will respond to my queries?
He asked himself;
All are lost in their unremitting work
Not a moment for anyone even to blink. (79)

Finding a little respite
Amidst the sea of humanity,
He starts selling the berry fruits
Brought all the way from home,
The large size juicy fruits
Allure everyone looking at them. (80)

Eventually an artisan was spotted
Who was nostalgic
About his home, sweet home
And was in a pensive mood;
He was exclaiming within
Alas! such a juicy fruit
Would have ripened
In my home garden too
In good number
(Where am I?
And where are those juicy fruits?) (81)

He (the artisan) looks at the face
Of young Dharmapada

Bishu Maharana, Dharmapada's father enquires of him his name, name of the village he has come from and other details to ascertain his identity.

Selling the fruits;
Is speechless with emotion
He broods over deep within,
But unable to find the reason
As to why he is struck with
Such uncanny filial love at his sight. (82)

He is curious to listen to his words,
He is filled with an untold delight;
He looks at Balia, the domestic pet

All doubts are set at rest; father and son are united and embrace each other.

From within the inner recesses of his heart
He feels as if someone is signaling
That the lad is the torch bearer of truth
And for him, his hour of reckoning
Has finally arrived. (83)

He enquires his name,
The name of the family
And the village
And all relevant details;
Finally, truth unfolds itself,

The suspense ends
The mystery is resolved
The fruit seller is none
Other than his own son.
Overwhelmed with affection
He embraces and kisses him,
The lad falls at his father's feet. (84)

The duo depart to the artisan's camp,
They exchange many pleasant thoughts
And share many warm moments;
Though at the peak of his ecstasy
The father is also in a hurry
And tells the son
That he has to rush
To the place of his work
If not, (he) may have to soon lose his head. (85)

Perplexed by his father's words
Dharmapada is keen and eager to know
The cause of such anxiety and concern;
The father is overpowered by grief,
Tears start trickling down his cheeks
And he remains for a moment
Speechless and dumbstruck. (86)

After a while

He regains composure
And says,
"It was my good fortune
That I could meet you
At the terminal phase of my life;
This is nothing but the outcome
Of accumulated virtues of my previous birth
And I feel indeed elated!" (87)

He then explains at length
The cause of his concern;
At the happy hour
Of their much cherished union,
"The work of construction (of the temple)
Has gone on
At a frantic pace
For long twelve years.
The lead, however, could not be fixed
At the temple top,
It could not as yet be sealed
Despite best efforts (of the artisans)
With all their devotion united." (88)

"A restless king
Who is intensely agitated and grieved,
Has decreed
That all artisans will lose their heads

If the lead is not fixed
Atop the temple in two days,
If the temple work is not complete
And nothing is left unfinished." (89)

"Of the two, one day is about to end
And only one more day will be left;
The artisans are clueless and in a fix
As to how to achieve this uncommon feat,
They are struck by despair and grief." (90)

The father elaborated further,
"Nobody knows
Where the fault lies,
Whether it is in the foundation
Which was laid in the heart of the river,
(Whether it lies
In wrong calculation of the center of gravity)
Or, whether,
It is due to
The anger of Lord Sun, (the king of planets)
(For some inexplicable reason)
Or, whether,
It is due to some (unpardonable) crime
That has been committed by someone else?" (91)

Every time the lead (chuda)

Is lifted to be fixed atop the temple,
It comes crashing down.
All efforts have ended in smoke;
If the chuda is not fixed on the kalas,
The temple construction will not finish.
All artisans are totally at a loss
To find a way out of this (mind boggling)
impasse." (92)

The father further continued,
"The king has also commanded
That a magnet be fixed
To the crown of the temple at the top;
All enemy ships going into the sea
Will thereby be attracted
And get eventually destroyed." (93)

"The twelve hundred artisans
One is as deft as the other,
All are adept in fine arts
With masonry and sculpture ingrained
In their veins and arteries.
They have to their credit
Countless temples, palaces, bridges and forts
As also numerous human settlements." (94)

"Each one is endowed

With the best of ingenuity and skill
All have set themselves heart and soul
To construct the chuda (dadhinauti),
And have it fixed
But alas!
Whenever the chuda is made and carried
To be fixed at the top of the kalas
It comes crashing down;
The hope of temple's completion
Remains a distant dream.
The artisans are at their wit's end
And have resigned themselves
To their inexorable fate". (95)

"Tonight will end,
Tomorrow the Sun will rise,
On the day after
The Sun will also rise
But only to witness
Destruction of the entire artisan race." (96)

"The artisans will meet
In the evening to deliberate,
To find a way out of the deadlock.
I have to leave (to participate in the parleys);
Having travelled a long journey
You would no doubt be feeling exhausted

You may, therefore, without any worry
Eat, sleep and rest. (97)

Seeing his father's plight
Dharmapada starts reflecting within himself,
With a sense of utter disbelief
And questions himself
Is this really going to happen?
Would the king Narasimha Deva
Be so cruel and heartless
That he would have
All the artisans beheaded? (98)

He further reflects within,
"The artisans of Utkal
Are unmatched in their dexterity and skill;
With the collective wisdom and insight
Which they represent,
Can any work, howsoever intricate,
Be left unfinished? (99)

Dharmapada speaks,
"O, father!
If you have no reservation
Please permit me
To accompany you
To the assembly of artisans;

Dharmapada attends the assembly of the artisans along with his father. He listens intently to the arguments and counter arguments going on among the artisans till late hours of the night, the discussion centering around as to how to seal the temple top.

I am keen and eager
To meet and listen to them.
I would love to learn
Complicated secrets of sculpture
From the twelve hundred artisans
Who undoubtedly are the pride of our clan." (100)

The father agreed
And together
They instantly left for the meeting place.
The twelve hundred artisans
Well versed in sculptural knowledge
Deliberated at length;
The art of construction
Of the temple and chariot,
The way the magnet
As desired by the king
Is to be fixed at the temple top. (101)

One statement is countered by another,
One argument is being outsmarted by the other;
The assembly continued till midnight
But the deliberations ended unsettled.
Seeing no light at the end of the tunnel
The artisans gave up all hopes of life. (102)

Before the assembly came to a close

Dharmapada rose from his seat,
He took the floor with folded hands
And with all humility
He spoke in a soft but resilient voice. (103)

"If Lord Jagannath
Residing at Neelachal Dham
Is true to Himself,
Take it from me
That no calamity
Will ever befall
On any one of our artisans." (104)

"If Lord Lingaraj
Installed in the heart of Ekamra Kanan
Is truly founded
On the mosaic of Truth
And Righteousness,
Take it from me
He will never put up with such infamy
Against the community
Of such famed artisans." (105)

"If Goddess Biraja
Would have truly emerged
From the sacrificial fire
Amid the chanting of hymns

And that of the four Vedas
Which reverberated
The message of divinity
Across the length and breadth
Of this holy land,
The twelve hundred artisans
Take it from me
Will not be beheaded
(For, such an inhuman act
Will be nothing
But a travesty of truth and justice"). (106)

He continued,
"I am a mere child
An ordinary mortal,
But (luckily for me)
I have been born
As a descendant of Lord Viswakarma
(Who is the divine builder)
And I belong to your clan;
If only
I have the gracious permission
Of my revered senior artisans
I shall attempt to seal the temple top." (107)

"And I am confident, he said,
That I shall succeed

In fixing the lead at the temple top
On the last and the most crucial hour.
This is my firm belief and conviction
I beseech you for this kind gesture (of permission)
I am only a humble servant at your feet." (108)

The assembly of artisans
Listened to the words
Of Dharmapada
With rapt attention
And utter disbelief;
Being quite astounded
They raised several queries:
"Is this ever credible?
Is it ever possible and achievable?
As the experience reveals
Every child,
On account of age and temperament
As also lack of sufficient exposure
To the grim realities of life
Tends to be immature
And fickle-minded,
It is difficult to accept
Such a bold and firm assertion
Coming from a twelve-year-old child." (109)

A sensitive artisan from the assembly got up
And spoke thus:
"If such a feat can be accomplished
In less than a day
By a twelve-year-old child
(What could not be achieved by all of us in
years),
It is much better
That all the artisans
Deserve to lose their heads." (110)

Yet another artisan got up
And made a statement
In a slightly different tone,
"Time being the essence
(In handling a crisis)
This is not the time
For expression of envy and ego;
Such vanity and arrogance
At this critical hour
Are unbecoming of us
(And will not take us anywhere).
If the unfinished task
Is accomplished,
Regardless of who does it,
It will uphold
The prestige, dignity and esteem

Of the entire clan of artisans.
There should be no scope
For any calumny against anyone." (111)

Someone else from the assembly
Made a counter statement,
"If accomplishment of the unfinished task
Is not kept a guarded secret
And if the information leaks out
As to who accomplished the rare feat,
The boy will no doubt
Be honoured by the royal court
By tying a 'saree' on his head,
While the twelve hundred artisans
Are destined to be beheaded. (112)

Such arguments and counter arguments
Continued for a while
Taking a heavy toll of time;
Finally an elderly artisan got up and said,
"This boy belongs to the clan of artisans,
If by the sheer grace of God
He accomplishes
What has remained unfinished
And an unresolved mystery
Gets resolved,
It will only add

To the prestige and honour
Of all the artisans.
It is of no consequence
If in the process
We have to lose our heads." (113)

He further said,
"Do not for a moment
By any stretch of your imagination
Attribute doubt and disbelief
To the firm resolve of this child.
Unsuspected and infinite indeed
Are the merit, ability and talent
Which lie hidden in every child
Which are independent of age
And which manifest themselves
With divine blessings.
Ordinary mortals
With average intelligence
Cannot sense
What they are capable of
Performing and accomplishing,
For which there is no barrier
Like one's age or experience." (114)

The old artisan further continued,
"Truth manifests itself

In the personality of every child,
A new strength and vitality
Emerges from the body of such a child
Which makes the impossible possible
(And the unachievable achievable too)
With the blessings of the God almighty." (115)

He further asked:
"Haven't you heard of Dhruba and Prahlada,
The celebrities of puranic lore?
Such characters are true to life
And not figments of imagination (of a poet);
A young child will doubtless
Accomplish the seemingly unachievable
If it is so divinely ordained." (116)

"Haven't you heard of Abhimanyu,
The Pandav prince of incomparable prowess
Who single handed fought
With grit, determination and courage
The seven warriors of Mahabharat
Who combined to kill him;
Abhimanyu, the young warrior
Remains incomparable till date
As he bravely fought till the last moment
And was brutally killed by deceit." (117)

"Haven't you heard of Shuka Muni
Who had acquired
Unparalleled spiritual knowledge (of the
'Brahman')
(Who never forgot to repeat
What he listened to like a parrot),
Right at the moment of his birth." (118)

Please remember, he continued,
"O, members of my clan!
Childhood is a stage in the cycle of life
Which is tender and formative
(And impressionable too),
It passes in due course
To adolescence, youth and adulthood.
Every child, as he crosses
The threshold of childhood
Acquires the maturity and sensibility,
Dexterity and skill of an adult,
Like the rising Sun of the morning
Which hides the intense midday heat." (119)

"Since only a day and night are left
(Take the bull by its horns)
Decide what is required to be done.
There is no time to be wasted
Either by way of dithering or vacillation

Far less procrastination and indecision
(As they won't take us anywhere)." (120)

"It is singularly our good fortune
That this boy has arrived on the scene
In the nick of time;
Prudence will complement providence
If we leave the unfinished task to him
Let this be our unanimous choice." (121)

The twelve hundred artisans
After a lot of deliberation
And hesitation
Reached the final decision
And spoke,
"Let him first go around
And minutely observe
The architecture of the temple
Throughout tomorrow. However,
All artisans will concentrate
On the unfinished task
And if they do not succeed,
They will surrender
And leave everything to the child
At the close of the crucial day indeed!." (122)

Bravo Bravo

All exclaimed and commended Dharmapada,
The fiercely independent spirited
(For his open and robust mind).
The assembly came to an end
The despondent artisans departed
With a pale face, to their respective camps
Only to resume their work the next day." (123)

4.

The next day
Dharmapada goes around
Surveys the technique and style
Of construction of the temple.
He minutely scans and scrutinises
The foundation, platform, pillars, joints and angles
From beginning to the end. (124)

In a bid to atone
The sins of their (past) lives
The twelve hundred artisans
Engaged themselves with full attention
To the unfinished task;
As the day came to an end
And the Sun set
They heaved a sigh of despair
As the chuda could not be fixed

Dharmapada starts working on the temple top by way of scrutinizing the foundation, platform, pillars, joints and angles of the temple after seeking permission from the artisans to do so.

On the kalas of the temple
And the top could not be sealed
Before expiry of the fateful night.
The exasperated artisans
Gave up their food, sleep and rest,
Out of grave anxiety
And end of their wits. (125)

Dharmapada spoke
To the assembly of artisans,
"I have gone around
And have studied
The architecture of the temple,
The foundation, platform, pillars, joints and
angles;
And now with your benign permission,
I shall begin my mission.
God willing,
The temple top can be fixed
Before the night ends
And the Sun rises." (126)

Please do, O, dear!
Please commence the unfinished task
And do not delay (even for a moment),
Said so without hesitation
All the twelve hundred artisans

In one single chorus and unison. (127)

While blessing Dharmapada
Through a loud chorus
They also exclaimed,
"Let the ambition of the king
Be fulfilled once and for all.
Let the glory of
The twelve-year-old son of an artisan
Be made known all over with renown. (128)

5.

Dharmapada climbed to the temple top
And started work in right earnest,
With single minded
Devotion and concentration.
The artisans on the other side
Were lost in mixed feelings of joy,
Of fruition and apprehension,
And an unpremeditated trepidation. (129)

That the king
Will doubtless come to know
Who has fixed the temple top;
He will doubtless honour him
By tying a 'saree' on his head.
Dharmapada's hour of crowning glory

Dharmapada eventually succeeds in sealing the temple top by putting the Dadhinauta (Chuda) on the top of the Kalas of the temple.

Will only herald the artisan's hour of doom.
(130)

The only silver lining
Which is in sight
Is that the temple top will be fixed
Bringing the construction work to a close;
Being mortally scared for their lives,
The anxiety and uncertainty in their minds
Compounded by fear and insecurity
(Arising out of)
the unforeseen shape of things. (131)

As they re-assembled
To count and recount the dreadful night,
Their minds loaded with
Thoughts of the impending calamity
The temple top got fixed
Imparting it the much-needed visibility. (132)

All the twelve hundred artisans
Intensely gazed at the temple top
With mixed feelings of
Amazement and jubilation
And simultaneous disbelief and concern.
Having accomplished the unfinished task
Dharmapada climbed down

The artisans express both admiration and surprise over Dharmapada's unique feat, tinged with unfounded fears and apprehension that while the young artist will receive royal recognition for his splendid success, they will be beheaded as ordered by the king.

And presented himself in their midst
Before the onset of dawn. (133)

6.

Dharmapada is lauded and cheered,
But the outer excitement and joy (of artisans)
Did not hide
The inner fear and gloom.
Dharmapada asked them thus:
"What is it, O, my revered elders!
That has overtaken all of you
For which you appear to be
So indifferent and faceless." (134)

"This is a moment of fulfilment,
He said,
Which should bring happiness and joy
Instead, the natural inner delight
Gets overshadowed
By the sudden cover
Of darkness and despair outside.
Why is it
That an untimely dew has fallen
On the face of the lovely lotus
Which is half-revealed and half-concealed?" (135)

An old artisan speaks
On behalf of others
In a husked tone and measured words,
"The temple top is fixed,
The temple work is now complete,
Your fame will no doubt
Spread far and wide
But we would be beheaded
As already commanded (by the king). (136)

Dharmapada interrupted him thus:
"It is futile to prolong this debate.
Of what consequence is that name
And all the honour associated (therewith)
If twelve hundred artisans
Representing twelve hundred petals (of glory)
Would wither away in wilderness
Before blossoming
To the flower of their full fame."(137)

He continued further:
"I am the son of an artisan,
I am only a humble progeny
Of the clan of twelve hundred artisans
I am their humble minion." (138)

Dharmapada reacts to their strange feelings, allays their fears and apprehensions, assures and re-assures them that there will be no threat to their lives. He a total stranger to the place, unknown to everybody, will depart from the scene and carve out his destiny in his own way.

"The entire credit", he continued further,
"For the work of this grand temple
Which has now come to a logical close,
Goes to all the twelve hundred artisans.
Where indeed is my humble contribution?" (139)

He further said,
"Whatever work was done (by me)
Is on account of
The blessings and direction
Of the senior members of my clan.
By giving such a direction
You have reposed in me
Your trust and confidence;
Of what use is this life
Lingering for me
If you have to lose
yours in ignominy." (140)

He further added,
"Please know it for certain
That the twelve hundred artisans
Are my illustrious progenitors;
The same blood which flows
In their arteries and veins
Also flows in those of mine.
I am one of them

And not one outside their fold,
Attuned to them in body, mind and spirit.
I assure you
Come what may,
To your lives
There will be no threat."(141)

He continued further,
"Nobody knows my name here
Nobody will ever know
Since I am a total stranger.
Before the night ends
And the day dawns
I shall carve out my own destiny
In my own hands
In my own way." (142)

He continued further,
"Nobody will ever come to know
How the temple top was fixed,
Neither the king
Nor his Minister and chief architect
Will ever come to know the truth.
So, why are you so upset
Since, to your lives
There will be no threat." (143)

"Only one quarter of the night is left
Please go back to your respective camps
O, my revered artisans!
For food, sleep and rest (in peace).
I bid farewell to all of you
I offer my humble obeisance at your feet." (144)

7.

The artisans departed
To their respective camps;
Dharmapada returned
To the camp of his father
And sought his permission thus,
"O, father !
if you do not think it otherwise,
If you do not feel threatened,
Please tell me
Who are you liable for,
Your son? Or
Twelve hundred artisans?
On your answer to my question
Would hinge
The deliverance of the members of your clan." (145)

The father feels instantly puzzled
And at a loss to comprehend
The meaning of

The awkward question of the son
Which is also quite a riddle,
His mind is laden with
So many vicious thoughts.
When a human being
Is in the midst of such deep crisis
He/she does not know
To which side he/she belongs. (146)

Dharmapada looks at the plight of his father
And says in a soft and tender voice,
"Let the twelve hundred artisans live
And you give me up for ever." (147)

He said
"This world is an illusion
Everyone here is deluded,
No one knows
Who is the father
And who is the son.
That life alone
Is worthy and meaningful
Which is consecrated
For sustenance and protection
Of the lives of women and men
who are the most precious
Objects in God's creation." (148)

He continued,
"This is what has been said
By our illustrious sages and seers;
If on one side
It becomes necessary
To sacrifice oneself
For the sake of (protection and sustenance)
many,
There should be
No hesitation to do so
However compelling or overpowering
May be
The bonds of love on the other side." (149)

He further added:
"The good human beings
Without getting worried,
Always sacrifice
The clan or community for the village.
They sacrifice the village
For the good of the nation;
They may (eventually) have to
Sacrifice the nation
For the welfare of humankind,
They may do so
Without any hesitation" (150)

He further continued,
"The twelve hundred artisans
Are my progenitors.
They constitute our lineage;
They are like garlands of
Fragrant flowers around our neck,
Let them live
At the cost of my life,
Wipe me out
From your thoughts forever. (151)

"Give up your blind attachment (for me),
We will not meet again in this life.
Bless and permit me to leave
At this very moment." (152)

The father (Bishu Maharana) said,
"Twelve years have rolled by
Since I left my hearth and home,
You were then only four months old
In your mother's womb.
I had no inkling
Whether it was a boy or a girl
Or, whether there was any miscarriage,
I did not get a single moment
Then or even now
To think about my offspring." (153)

"You came
At the most appropriate moment
And took the cudgel
On your shoulders
Entirely of your own volition,
You were absolutely confident
Of your insight, skill and acumen,
As also sanguine of your success
And made in no time
An impossible act possible." (154)

"Who, or any other
Ordinary mortal like me
With limited fortune
Is fortunate to have
A son of your merit, intelligence and talent?" (155)

"Your advent on the scene
Was like a flash of lightning,
Having arrived with such a flash.
Why do you allow it to diminish
And eventually disappear
And lose your own identity?
Is this the (expected) outcome
Of such a splendid fortune
(Of meeting you)?
What have I done

To deserve such an irony of fate
By parting company with you
Within hours
Of our much cherished union?" (156)

"In which previous births of mine,
In whose eating plate
Did I throw some dust
To be cursed to suffer
Such an ignominious fate?" (157)

"From whose
Two palms of hands held together
Did I steal some wealth
And shackled his hands
(Or fettered his feet)
To deserve such a cursed fate?" (158)

"My previous births
Have been laden with demerits
And unpardonable sins;
If that were not so
You would not be
Leaving me like this,
Reducing me
To the level of
A sightless emotional wreck

After illuminating my path,
Even if it was for a moment,
By a streak of rare light. (159)

"The twelve hundred artisans
Are no doubt our kith and kin
Who have sustained our lineage,
But I do not need them
(at this hour of my life).
If, instead, I had a son
Of your merit, ability and talent,
The pride and esteem of our clan
Will remain ever intact. (160)

"You are one in ten millions
Who is ever keen and eager
To uphold the pride and esteem of his clan;
Whose qualities of head and heart
As they unfold
Become the pride of the world,
Yet another (like you)
Is not to be seen again. (161)

The son reacted
Out of concern
And rather swiftly
"O, father!

Please do not proceed further,
No use to have such endless musings.
I have made up my mind
And I want to leave once for all;
It is getting rather late (for me),
I must leave before the night ends
And before the day dawns. (162)

The father asks
With a lot of anxiety and concern
"Where do you want to go?
Would you remain safe and sound?
Would you remain alive in flesh and blood?
If you remain alive
Who knows when
We shall meet again.
Please do not hide
But unfold, O, my dear!
What is your true intention?" (163)

The son turns philosophical for a moment
And responds to his father's queries thus:
"O, father !
Life and death
Follow each other
(Like day and night)
In a ceaseless link;

For certain is death for the born
(And certain is birth for the dead),
They follow each other
Before or after
Rather incessantly without a break." (164)

He continued thus:
"To die like a coward
Does not add
To a woman or man's valour;
Only one
Who strives for the good of others
And abdicates all
That he/she owns and cherishes
And dies in the process
Of incessant and selfless action
Remains truly illustrious
As also a good human being." (165)

He further said:
"Remember, O, father !
Human life
Is not a calendar collection
Of years, months, days and hours,
Every human being
Lives for action
(Which is purposive and meaningful)

And such action
Is only the true measuring rod of life." (166)

He continued further,
"A streak of fire
Which burns bright
And which through its radiant flame
Disseminates heat and light
In all directions;
It destroys darkness and gloom
And brightens the universe
With its blazing rays,
Even if it burns for a moment
And gets extinguished after
It establishes its eternal worth
To burn, illuminate and disseminate (light)." (167)

"Of what use, he continued,
Is another fire
Which may be smouldering
For thousands of years,
But does not burn brightly
Even for a moment
(Except emitting a lot of smoke)."(168)

The son emphatically added further:
"Please take it from me

O, father!
I say it for certain
That we will not meet again,
Since life and death
Are only two sides of the same coin
Not much different from each other.
Why, therefore, do you have to raise
The same issue again and again?" (169)

Then he said:
"It is my good fortune
That I came here,
Met you at the right time
And made good use of
Whatever little skills
I had imbibed in my childhood
In the deft hands of my mother;
Whatever I had learnt
From the priceless treasure
Of 'Shilpa Shastra' kept at our home
And succeeded
In sealing the temple top." (170)

He continued:
"What great pleasure
is to be derived by me,
Even after fixing the temple top

If twelve hundred artisans
Who belong to the same clan
As I do,
Are to suffer so much ignominy and defamation
And eventually meet
a most inglorious and tragic fate?" (171)

He further said with a lot of anguish,
"How would my acclaim in the royal court
Further boost my reputation
When all the credit, honour and fame
Earned by the twelve hundred artisans
After their 'blood, sweat and tears' for years;
And the wealth
Associated with that fame
Will be coming to an end
With their tragic death
And drenched in their blood?" (172)

"What ghastly picture
Will future history paint?
In what colour and brush?
That I would be walking
In the royal Court
With 'Saree' and 'Sherpa'[7]

---

7 Sarees are worn by women but in old days (during the days of monarchy in particular), it was customary to tie one's head with a saree as a mark of honour as also a mark of recognition of one's worth and contribution. Same is true of 'Sherpa'

Tied as turban to my head on one side
And my proud ancestors,
Torch bearers of a lofty lineage,
be put to death alongside?" (173)

He continued further:
"Assuming I would not have come
And the temple top would not have been fixed,
And all the artisans would have been beheaded;
They would no doubt have died,
But would not have suffered
So much calumny, agony and shame
that have now arisen in their minds
On account of me laying my hands
on the temple top."(174)

"I do not want" he continued,
"That our hoary tradition
Of incomparable artistry and skill
Of the proud artisans of Utkal
Should carry the taint
Of such defamation." (175)

"It behoves of you
O, my father!
And it will be most appropriate
In the situation

In which we are now placed
That you sacrifice me
With a clean and detached mind and pure heart
For the sake of our
Distinguished tradition and lineage." (176)

"Haven't you heard, O, father!
That great story of incredible pathos and piety
Woven with a sense of extraordinary justice
As depicted in the great epic 'Mahabharat?" (177)

A pigeon being chased by a hawk
Took shelter in the lap of Sibi,
The kind-hearted king of Kashi.
The king felt pity for the innocent pigeon
Who being chased by one
Infinitely
More powerful
Took shelter with the king
In fear and pain. (178)

This happened at a time
while the king
Was performing a sacrificial fire.
This put him in a terrible fix.
If he failed to protect the pigeon
(Who is helpless and in need of protection)

The outcome of the sacrificial fire will go waste.
(179)

At the same time,
If the king kills the hawk
(He was capable and obliged
to do so as part of his 'rajadharma'
to protect the weak)
Who was chasing the pigeon,
He will no doubt be charged
With the crime of
Committing a grave sin
By murdering a living being
Who was hungry
By depriving it of its natural prey. (180)

Unable to find a way
Between the two horns of a dilemma,
The king stood
Between the predator and the victim
And appealed to the good sense
And conscience of the hawk thus:
"O, king of birds!
I am willing to fulfil
Any wish which you may have,
But I beseech you
Please spare the life of this pigeon

Who is innocent and helpless."(181)

The hawk declined the offer
And said it was hungry
And that the pigeon was its normal food,
And, further, that he was not
In need of any wealth
And, therefore,
Had no other wish to be fulfilled. (182)

He, however, gave an alternative offer
And told the king
That if he was so keen
To save the life of the pigeon,
With such magnanimous intent
He should cut off
An equal amount of flesh
From his body (as that of the pigeon's). (183)

The king instantly agreed to the offer
And blocks of flesh were removed
From his body
And put in the weighing balance
with the pigeon. (184)

Every time blocks of flesh were removed
From the king's body

And put in the weighing balance,
They did not measure
Up to the weight of the pigeon. (185)

One after the other
Pieces of flesh were cut
From the body of the king
And put in the weighing balance;
The pigeon, however, weighed more
Than the weight of the king's flesh. (186)

Eventually, (when King Sibi was about to bleed
to death)
This turned out to be
A supreme test of his
Magnanimity, munificence and sacrifice
And he emerged victorious.
The hawk (a God in disguise) gave up its prey
And lauded the king
For his resounding victory,
Showered divine blessings on him
And departed (from where it had come). (187)

Dharmapada continued
"Through such an act
Of unparalleled self-abnegation and sacrifice,
The great king Sibi acquired

In this world and after
The cherished four objects
Which all and sundry mortals crave
(Dharma, Artha, Kama and Moksha)." (188)

He continued thus:
"This world is like
A great entrance room to a temple,
Women and men are worshippers
Who get a sacrifice performed by a priest
(On payment of an honorarium).
They are all seekers
Of the fruits of their action (through a sacrifice).
Only those women and men
Eventually emerge victorious
Who (like king Sibi) sacrifice their own lives
For others
(Instead of being desirous of the fruits of their
action)." (189)

"You must also have heard
The immortal story of Sage Dadhichi
Who sacrificed himself
By self-immolating his mortal frame
So that the bones from his dead body
Could be used for making 'bajrastra'
(a divine weapon called 'thunderbolt')

With which Vritrasura,
The infamous demon
Who had usurped the land
And tortured living beings,
(By draining the earth of all its water
And causing large scale drought)
Could be killed by Indra,
The God of Devas." (190)

He continued,
"We have, O, father!
Stories of
So many good and great human beings
Who have sacrificed their lives
For the good of humanity;
Such sacrifice and self-abnegation
Bring a rare fullness to life.
They also bring
Life's eternal consciousness
Amidst the pangs of
Decay, destruction and death." (191)

Dharmapada continued,
"The buds of life
Blossom in the midst of lakes of love.
They spread their fragrance
In the air all around

And attain the status of a full bloom.
Lord Sun through his bright light
Lights and enlivens the world,
Protects and sustains the universe
By removing darkness;
Its rays emit a gentle smile
Which is also lovely and pleasing
(And which bring to life
Peace, serenity and bliss)." (192)

"The twelve hundred artisans
Have been eagerly waiting
To hear from you
Your final decision
About them in relation to me;
The moment you severe
The ties of your blind love (for me)
They will feel relieved and redeemed." (193)

"Please look at their face, O, father!
(They are full of anxiety, depression and gloom)
Give up, therefore, your infatuation with me.
Think for a moment
That I have fallen and died
From the temple top.
My head, heart and bones
Have all been severed

And crushed to pieces
And that I am no longer
Alive in flesh and blood." (194)

"Please also think
For a moment, O, father!
That I have not been born
But, instead, have died
Inside the womb of my mother
Due to miscarriage
Or any other accident.
Looking at this beautiful temple,
Looking at the illustrious artisans
Who have erected it
By their 'blood, sweat and tears'
And have carried it to a logical close.
Please give up this faint-heartedness
And the uncalled for sadness
Associated therewith." (195)

You may, O, father!
Be thinking,
How without me
Our dynasty will be protected?
Please think for a while
Which dynasty has remained
Permanent on earth

And what purpose it has served?" (196)

"So many good human beings, O, father!
Have come and departed,
Having achieved the unachievable,
Have also perished
With the currents of time,
Where is their dynasty?
All that remains
And all that is remembered
Is only their good work,
Contribution and reputation
What they have left behind
On the sands of time." (197)

"One sacrifices oneself
To pave the way
For protection and redemption of others;
The one who sacrifices oneself
In essence,
Promotes fulfilment of self
Through the happiness and well-being of others.
This is the eternal law of creation." (198)

"Let the so-called dynasty come to an end,
But let the class of artisans
As a collective entity

Survive, flourish and expand.
Let this be adopted
As a sublime principle of life,
Let the Sun temple at Konark
Sing the saga
Of your most virtuous collective sacrifice." (199)

"Haven't you heard, O, father!
The story of sacrifice
By many a kind and compassionate soul,
Who in a bid
To stand up
To the dictates of 'Truth'
Did not hesitate
Even to sacrifice their own son(s)
As an act of benediction for others
Without any remorse or lament
Even for a moment?" (200)

"One qualifies to be called a true hero
Who lawfully discharges the duty
That befalls one's lot
With courage, valour and dedication.
History has recorded
Many such heroic exploits.
They (those heroic characters),
Like Shree Rama Chandra, the warrior

Who built a bridge across the Indian ocean,
Are able to build bridges
Across the ocean of the universe. (201)

Dharmapada enters into a long debate with his father about the importance of preserving the pride, esteem, pursuit of excellence in skills and need for physical survival of the 1200 artisans who are an asset to the State vis-a-vis his own life as an ordinary mortal and the futility of the talk behind preserving the Progeny, bids adieu to his father.

We have met only for a day,
Why do you, O, father!
Fall victim to such delusion
Of uncalled for attachment
That amounts to infatuation?
Please give up such weakness
That is illusory,
Please show your true manliness
By not going
Against the interests of our clan. (202)

"O, father ! say graciously
That you are liable only
For the twelve hundred artisans
And not liable for your son;
Let this story
Be remembered for all time to come,
Throughout the world
And let me bid goodbye."(203)

"O, father !
The dark night is coming to a close,
My (chosen) path looks straight and clear.
Bless me
And accept this obeisance
Of mine forever." (204)

8.

Having said this,
Dharmapada took particles of dust
From his father's feet
And smeared his forehead.
The old man (Bishu Maharana)
Was speechless,
Being overtaken by sadness.
Tears trickled down his cheeks,
He gave his last kiss
On Dharmapada's face
As a mark of his silent bliss. (205)

The son departed,
And the father
Overwhelmed with an inconsolable grief,
Unable to bear the pangs of separation
(After the much-cherished union),
Fell down unconscious
Writhing in physical and mental anguish. (206)

The dark night has not fully departed,
The dark cover from her body
Has not been fully shed,
The dawn with its soft and slender smile
Has not unfolded,
The eastern sky is not yet fully open

But looks decorated and brilliant,
Tinged with the light dark reddish colour
Of the rays of the forthcoming rising Sun. (207)

The soft and gentle breeze
Blows over the river (Chandrabhaga),
The gentle waves lash the shore;
Away in the not-too-distant forest
The bird Kumbhatua[8] sings,
Announcing the arrival
Of the dawn and daylight. (208)

At this hour of the break of the dawn
Dharmapada moved with brisk steps
(And with determination)
He climbed the chariot of the temple,
Through temporary stairs
And quickly climbed to the top. (209)

8 'Kumbhatua' is a bird which usually sings during pre-dawn hours to announce the arrival of the dawn and daylight (Usually it sings during or little before the close of the last quarter of the night)

9.

A vast mass of sands
Lie scattered in all directions.
In the front
Lies the limitless expanse of the blue sea
Its perennial waves
Are incessantly lashing the shore,
The latter wears a deserted and silent look. (210)

Dharmapada sings:
"O, Supreme Creator!
You are pure, luminous, stainless, spotless and bright;
You represent the whole universe,
You are the primordial force behind creation,
You have pervaded the whole world,
Around all movable and immovable objects.
In you flows
The milk of human kindness,
You are the eternal abode
Of happiness and love.
For one and all
Victory to you
O, my Lord of the Universe!" (211)

You are formless and shapeless
And incorporeal,

You are the very sheet anchor
Of the Universe,
(And of the mundane human existence)
You manifest yourself
Both in the interior and the exterior;
You are the master creator of the whole world,
You provide refuge to those
Who are shelter-less,
As also helpless
Victory to you
O, my Lord of the Universe!" (212)

The tender heart of Dharmapada
Identified itself
With the vast canopy of a limitless entity;
He got over the feeling
That he was birth-less,
And thought (for a moment)
That he and the universal life
Were one and indivisible. (213)

It appeared for a moment
As if the whole universe compressed itself
And got subsumed in that tiny heart;
The flow of nectar underlying the divine music,
Emerging from the innermost recesses
Of Dharmapada's heart,

Integrated the inner and outer Universe
Into one larger whole. (214)

With one body, one mind and one heart,
Aligning himself with the rhythm of universal music,
With pristine purity
And single-minded devotion
He (Dharmapada) sang
With a lot of zest and joy;
Victory to you
O, my Lord of the Universe! (215)

Above him
Lay the vast expanse
Of a limitless blue sky,
Studded with stars
And beautifully decorated.
From his unsullied heart
Emerged lofty thoughts
Which are extraordinary and sublime. (216)

The earth, sky and sea
Became one,
Endowed with one thought
Their multi-dimensionality
Faded into oblivion.

They all merged
Into one object
Which has no beginning and no end,
Which cannot be pierced,
Which is paramount and without remorse,
Which manifests itself
Into one great universal entity. (217)

Dharmapada sings again,
"O, my Lord!
The wind blows in the sky
All the time
Deriving its phenomenal strength
From your supreme (divine) self;
The ocean never crosses
Beyond its boundaries
Without your command,
Victory to you
O, my Lord of the Universe!" (218)

"O, my Lord!
Your effulgent divine light
Manifests itself
All the time
In the blue sky
Through heavenly bodies (stars and planets).
Only by your divine grace

The flowers blossom
in their resplendent glory
And spread their fragrance around,
Victory to you
O, my Lord of the Universe!" (219)

"O, my Lord!
The rivers, forests and mountains
Who combine in them
Both beautiful and vicious forms,
Take shelter under your (benign) glance.
The universal Goddess of learning
Sings paeans of your glory,
Victory to you
O, my Lord of the Universe!" (220)

"O, my Lord!
Your glory is infinite
It has no beginning and no end,
Your exquisite beauty
Is incomparable;
It is visible
In every layer of the earth,
Your magnificent
Kindness and compassion
Weave themselves
Into every animate and inanimate,

Every movable and immovable
Object of the Universe.
Victory to you
O, my Lord of the Universe!" (221)

"O, my Lord!
How can a tiny and ordinary mortal like me
Comprehend your pristine glory?
What language can I adopt
To sing the glory of your greatness?
Victory to you
O, my Lord of the Universe!" (222)

"O, my Lord!
That glory transcends
The limited boundaries of time and space,
It is incomprehensible
To ordinary mortals and even Gods.
It overflows with divine love,
It is unique and unparalleled.
Victory to you
O, my Lord of the Universe!" (223)

"O, my Lord!
You are higher than the highest,
You are greater than the greatest,
You represent the paramount,

The supreme and absolute.
I pray to you my Lord!
Please provide a little refuge
To me in the dust of your glorious feet;
Let your grand desire be fulfilled
Through this ordinary mortal.
Victory to you
O, my Lord of the universe!" (224)

"O, my Lord!
You have divinely inspired me,
You have infused in my heart
Your unbounded love and kindness
And divine inspiration.
O, the Ocean of compassion!
Please allow that love
To be carried to its logical close.
Victory to you
O, my Lord of the Universe!" (225)

"O, the Lord of my heart!
One who knows the minds of one and all,
The ins and outs of everyone.
Please bless me with that nectar of salvation,
What you have once demonstrated.
Victory to You
O, my Lord of the Universe!" (226)

"O, my dear Mother Chandrabhaga!
Please accept my greetings,
Please accept me
As an integral part of your (divine) being,
Please drown me with your motherly love,
Please merge (eternally)
My (mortal) being with you and the ocean
With the same unbounded affection
As that of my own mother
Whose depth cannot be easily measured." (227)

Thus singing 'Hari Hari' (O, Lord, O, Lord)
He plunged himself into the river;
There was no trace left
Of his mortal self,
It went deep inside the ocean bed. (228)

The very next day
The Sun rose
With all its resplendent glory,
And fully kissed
The temple top
In its entirety.
Nobody had any inkling
As to who had sealed
The temple top
At Konark. (229)

The mortal remains of Dharmapada,
His flesh and blood
Merged with
The rivers, forests and mountains,
In the depth of the seabed
The name of Dharmapada
Was totally devoured by the eternal devourer
(Kala).
The unforgettable was soon forgotten. (230)

The face of 'Truth'
Cannot, however, be hidden
(Even in a pot of gold);
It will reveal one day in its full form.
It is true
That there is no Dharmapada in flesh and blood
There are only the fragile remains of a temple
In its ruins
As a mute witness,
Dharmapada lives in legends. (231)

After offering prayers to the creator who is immanent, all pervasive, all-encompassing and infinitely merciful and also to river Chandrabhaga, Dharmapada jumps from the temple top into the river and the sea down below and sacrifices his life for the cause of holding the safety, security, dignity and esteem of the life of 1200 artisans.

Appendix

Both in the preface by the author of the original text 'Dharmapada' i.e. Utkalmani Pandit Gopabandhu Dash as also in the body of the text 'Dharmapada' itself, references have been made to certain places and characters (both puranic and historical). While translating the text from Oriya to English, it was felt necessary by the translator that a gist of these puranic/historical references should be provided for the benefit of the readers who did not have access to the original text due to the language barrier. The names of these places and characters and the outcome of puranic and historical research into them have been presented below in an alphabetical order such as:

- Abhimanyu
- (King) Anangabhim Deva III
- Badal
- Barbati Fort

- Biraja Kshetra and Temple
- (Sage) Dadhichi
- Dhruba
- Eklavya
- Jagadguru Adi Shankaracharya
- (King) Jajati Keshari
- (King) Indradyumna
- (King) Langula Narasimha Deva 1
- (Bhakta) Prahlad
- Sadashiva Samantray (Sibei Santra)
- Shuka Muni
- Sibi
- Sapta Matrukas

While a brief introduction has been given about King Sibi, sage Dadhichi and Maharaja Langula Narasimha Deva 1 at the appropriate place in the translated text, a more detailed description is being given in the appendix (in an alphabetical order) for the benefit of all our readers--Indian and foreign.

Abhimanyu

Abhimanyu is a character that appears in the Hindu epic 'Mahabharata'. Abhimanyu was born to the third Pandav prince Arjuna and Jadav princess Subhadra, who was also Lord Krishna's sister. Abhimanyu was raised by his maternal uncle i.e. Lord Krishna as his father

Arjuna along with his four brothers and wife - Panchal Princess Draupadi went into exile for 13 years after having lost the deceitful game of dice with Duryodhana, the Kaurava prince of Hastinapura and the wily Sakuni, Maharani Gandhari's brother and Duryodhana's uncle.

During exile (for 13 years) and exile incognito (for one year), at one time, the Pandava brothers have assumed different names and lived with Virata, the king of Matchya. Kichaka, the most powerful general of the king, once made inappropriate advances on Draupadi, who was under the guise of Sairindiri. After Bhima, disguised as a cook in the royal kitchen, killed Kichaka in a single duel, the Kaurava army invaded the Matchya kingdom. Arjuna, the third of the Pandav brothers, disguised as Brihannala (a transgender) and dance teacher of Uttara, the Princess was acting as the charioteer of the Prince of the Matsya Kingdom in this battle.

Since the Prince developed cold feet and was unable to fight, Arjuna took the arms on his behalf and defeated the Kaurava army. Virata asked Arjuna to marry his daughter Uttara. Since Arjuna had been Uttara's dance teacher in his disguise as the transgender Brihannala, he proposed her marriage with his son Abhimanyu and the marriage took place.

At the end of the exile including the exile incognito, when Lord Krishna was sent as an emissary to negotiate for a just and fair share of Hastinapur kingdom in favour of the Pandava brothers, Duryodhana, the wily prince and the usurper refused to part with any land, not even equivalent to the space occupied by the top of a needle, and the inevitable battle of Mahabharata took place at a place called 'Kurukshetra' (a district in present day Haryana State). On the thirteenth day of the battle, Drona, the general of the Kaurava army formed a 'Chakravyuha'. On this fateful day, however, Arjuna was diverted, rather deceitfully, to the south by the 'Trigarthas'. The 'Chakravyuha' was set up with a view to trapping the eldest Pandav prince Yudhisthira (taking advantage of the absence of Arjuna) so that the battle could come to an end and further bloodshed could be avoided.

As the story goes, when Abhimanyu was in his mother's womb, he had heard a conversation between his parents i.e. Arjuna and Subhadra about how to enter the 'Chakravyuha' but Subhadra fell asleep before Arjuna could complete the full story of the strategy to both enter and come out of the 'Chakravyuha'. So Abhimanyu only knew the first part of the story i.e. how to get into the 'Chakravyuha but was not familiar with the second part i.e. the strategy of getting out of it.

As the story in the epic 'Mahabharata' goes further, Abhimanyu enters the 'Chakravyuha' and kills Lakshman, the son of Duryodhana. Drona thereafter, under instructions of a furious Duryodhana, changed the strategy which in effect meant that the seven maharathis (great warriors) should combine to kill Abhimanyu by foul means, if necessary. Initially, Bhim, Nakul and Sahadeb, the three Pandav brothers accompanied Abhimanyu and protected him from behind but at a crucial stage, they were effectively stopped by Jayadrath, king of Sindh and an ally of Duryodhana. Drupada and Dhristadyumna who were allies of the Pandavas were also stopped from advancing further, leaving Abhimanyu all alone. Before reaching the centre, Abhimanyu killed many warriors but once he reached the centre of the 'Chakravyuha' he, contrary to the law of fairness in a war, was jointly attacked by Drona, Dushasana, Aswatthamma, Karna, Sakuni, Duryodhana, Kripacharya, Kritavarma and many others. He fought all of them single-handed and defeated most of them in a single combat.

Later, his divine 'Rudra bow' given to him by Arjuna (which had made him invincible), was destroyed by Karna; his chariot was also destroyed. Remaining undeterred, Abhimanyu displayed rare bravery by fighting with sword, mace and even a wheel of the chariot but eventually was killed by Dushasan's eldest son. The puranic character as described in the epic is an exemplary one representing all the virtues of a young warrior - brave, gentle, honest, large-hearted with tremendous will-power together with extraordinary prowess and martial genius.

(King) Anangabhim Dev 3 (1211-1238)

He was the son of king Rajraj Dev and queen Malwan Devi. When he ascended the throne in 1211, Bengal bordering Utkal was being governed by Muslim rulers. The Sultan of Bengal had established his supremacy and suzerainty by not accepting even the Mughal emperors of Delhi as his ruler. From an inscription available in Bateswar temple in Krishnapur village (Padampur Pargana of Cuttack), it appears that Anangabhim Dev 3 emerged victorious after successive battles with the Sultan of Bengal. He also conquered Sonepur by defeating the Kalchuri king of Ratanpur after which he got his daughter Chandrika Devi married to the prince of Kalchur - Paramardhi Deva and appointed him as the general of his army. With this brave prince as his general, he expanded his empire till the Krishna river in the South.

This is evident from the Kanchipuram inscription of the Queen (1230). During his reign, the city of Varanasi in the north was devastated due to Muslim invasion and the Kashi Viswanath temple was also destroyed. Anangabhim Dev 3 established 'Abhinab Varanasi' at Cuttack (known as Bidanasi of today). He got a number of temples constructed such as Purusottam temple at 'Abhinab Varanasi,' Cuttack (1231) and two temples of Lord Shiva namely Chitreswar and Bighneswar on the bank of river 'Mahanadi'. A large number of inscriptions such as two at Lingaraj temple of Bhubaneswar, four at Pataleswar temple at Puri, one at Bateswar temple of Padampur, Cuttack, two at Draksharam, two at Simanchal (now in Andhra Pradesh) and five at tortoise temple have been found.

These inscriptions (an admixture of Oriya and Sanskrit) present a clear picture about the reign of Anangabhim Dev 3. These are further supplemented by an important historical chronicle called 'Madala Panji'. According to the said chronicle, land reforms were taken up for the first time during the tenure of Anangabhim Dev 3. He was also instrumental in the construction of Barbati fort at Cuttack (which was both re-constructed and completed by Telenga Mukunda Dev (1559-1568). He was an extremely devout ruler, a lover of art, literature and sculpture and had established a number of institutions in conformity with the dictates of scriptures such as Vishnu Dharmottar Purana, Aditya Purana, Bamana Purana etc. The Ananta Vasudeb temple at Bhubaneswar was constructed by his daughter Chandrika Devi.

Badal

According to 'Padmawat,' composed by Malik Muhammad Jayase in 1589 AD, Badal served along with Gora, the king of Chittorgarh called Ratnasen or Ratan Singh, also known as the Rana of Chittorgarh in the early fourteenth century. According to the same 'Padmawat', Alauddin Khilji (1296 AD-1316 AD), the Sultan of Delhi attacked Chittorgarh to obtain Padmavati, the beautiful queen of Rana of Chittorgarh-Ratnasen. During a peace negotiation, Ratnasen invited Alauddin Khilji as a guest of the Rana inside the Chittorgarh Fort much against the advice of Gora and Badal. At the time of his departure, Alauddin Khilji deceitfully captures Ratnasen (who had come out of the fort to escort his guest as per Rajput tradition) and returns to Delhi. Before departure and while inside the fort as a guest of the Rana, he deceitfully catches a glimpse of the queen Padmavati. The queen seeks the help of Gora and Badal to free Ratnasen from the captivity of the Sultan of Delhi.

Disguised as Padmavati and her female companions, Gora and Badal enter the fort of Delhi, free Ratnasen, ensure that he is escorted safely to Chittorgarh but sacrifice their lives in a fierce but brave battle which ensues soon after the Sultan of Delhi discovers that he has been outwitted, the captive Rana has been released and taken away to Chittorgarh. Subsequently he invades Chittorgarh which is devastated in the battle with the Rana being treacherously killed and Padmavati along with all her companions observing 'Johar' or self-immolation.

While this is the story of character 'Badal' which has been referred to by the poet in the preface to 'Dharmapada', and a film captioned 'Padmavati (2018)' has also been made by Director Sanjay Leela Bhansali, the entire episode has been surrounded by disputes in terms of historical accuracy. These, however, leave the character 'Badal', his bravery and heroic sacrifice (which is the focal point of our reference) untouched.

Barbati Fort

From all available records, it appears that this is a thirteenth century fort whose initial construction was taken up by King Anangabhim Dev 3 (1211-1238) but whose construction was completed by Telenga Mukund Dev (1559-1568), the last Hindu king of Utkal. Situated at 20°29' 4.67' North85°51' 51.93' East about 8-kms away from the centre of Cuttack city. It is located at 14.62 meters above sea level with Mahanadi river in the North and Kathjodi river in the south. Spread over an area of 102 acres, the fort is square in design. It is surrounded on all sides with a stone paved moat of 10 meters width in the north and 20 meters width in the eastern and southern sides. As of now, the entire fort wall except the entrance is missing. The remains of the ruined fort have been declared as a protected site by the Archaeological Survey of India since 1915.

In 1568, Mukund Dev, the last Hindu king of Utkal lost the battle with Kalapahada, general to Suleman Karnani, the ruler of Bengal. Mukund Dev lost his life in a fierce fight at Gohiratikir near Jajpur and the city of Cuttack passed into the hands of the victor. Eight years later, it passed to the Mughal ruler Akbar, and eventually to the Maratha rulers in 1741. Odisha remained under their control till 1803, when it came under the British rule. At a relevant point of time, the Barbati Fort was being used as a prison for confinement of several illustrious personalities of the land.

Telenga Mukund Dev (1559-1568) got a nine storied mansion constructed inside the fort, which was well designed. The ground floor was for elephants, horses and camels. The second floor was meant for storing arms and ammunitions. The fort security guards were also accommodated in this floor. The third floor was meant for the housekeeping staff. The fourth floor was meant for masons, artisans and sculptors. The fifth floor was being used as the kitchen. The sixth floor was used for king's interviews with visitors. The seventh floor was meant for family functions as also for confidential record keeping. The eighth floor was being used for the harem and the top floor (ninth one) was meant for the king's bedroom.

Regretfully, today all that remains of the fort, once the pride of Utkal, is only an arched gateway and the eastern mound of the nine storied palace.

Biraja Kshetra and temple

The 'Biraja' temple dedicated to Goddess Biraja or Durga is one of the ancient Hindu temples located in Jajpur town, 125 kms from the State capital Bhubaneswar. At one time and during the reign of Somvanshi king Jajati Keshari (1024-1040 AD), this was the capital of Utkal called Jajatipur. The present temple was constructed in the 13th century. Biraja, the presiding deity of the temple, represents Shakti or Goddess Durga. Unlike the traditional Goddess Durga with eight hands, in Biraja temple, she has only two hands. In one she is seen piercing the chest of demon Mahisasura with a trident. Mahisasura has assumed the shape of a buffalo and Biraja has the trident in one hand and with the other hand, she is pulling the tail of the demon. The crown of Biraja has Ganesha, crescent moon and a shivalinga as distinct symbols.

The 'Brahmayamala tantra' has a hymn called 'Aadya stotra' dedicated to 'Shakti.' According to the said hymn, 'Vimala' is the Goddess representing 'Shakti' being worshipped at the Shree Jagannath temple at Puri and 'Biraja' at Biraja kshetra at Jajpur. According to tantra 'Chudamani,' the navel of 'Sati,' the daughter of 'Dakshya Prajapati' and wedded to Lord 'Shiva,' fell in Utkal kingdom. This area was also known as 'Biraja' kshetra after she consigned herself to the flames of the sacrificial fire (organised by her father) following disrespect shown to her husband at the gathering of guests invited for the sacrificial fire. Jagadguru Adi Shankaracharya in his 'Astadasha Shakti Peetha Stotram' describes the Goddess as 'Girija.' In tantra literature, the Odiyan Peetha is the same as 'Biraja Kshetra' located on the bank of river Baitarani, one of the major rivers of Odisha today.

At Biraja Kshetra, there is a separate shrine for Shree Baglamukhi Devi towards the right of Ma Biraja. This represents a unique form of 'Dasamahavidya' which is rarely found elsewhere.

'Navi Gaya' is yet another center of attraction and relevance in Biraja Kshetra. Just as 'Pitapuram' holds the 'Pada Gaya', the 'Siro Gaya' is found in Bihar, 'Navi Gaya' is found in Biraja Kshetra in the form of a well. Various forms of oblations to our ancestors in the form of 'Pinda Dana' and 'Tarpan' are performed here by a large number of Hindu devotees.

(Sage) Dadhichi

He is also known as Dadhyancha or Dadhyanga which is a conjunction of two words such as Dadhya (curd) and anch or anga (parts) meaning body parts deriving strength from curd. Sage Dadhichi is a central character in Hinduism. In 'Bhagabat Purana' he is known as the son of sage 'Atharva' and his wife 'Chiti', the former being the author of 'Atharva Veda'.

Dadhichi was also a master of 'Brahma Vidya' i.e. the knowledge of 'Brahma' or 'Supreme Spirit'. Sage Dadhichi was an ardent devotee of Lord 'Shiva' although he had utmost respect for Lord 'Vishnu' as well. As the story goes, Indra, the Chief of the Devas was once driven out of deva loka (kingdom of heaven) by a demon called 'Vritra'. The latter was the recipient of a boon which made him invincible to any known weapon. The demon also stole all the water in the world for his own use and for that of the demon army causing large scale drought in the earth all around. When Indra approached Lord 'Vishnu' to rescue him from this distress, he was told that only weapons made from the bones of Sage Dadhichi could kill Vritrasura. The sage was approached by the Devas led by Indra (who had once beheaded the sage as he felt insecure with Sage Dadhichi being a master of 'Brahmavidya') and made a fervent request for donation of his body so that the demon Vritra could be killed with the bajrastra (thunder) made out of his bones. The sage acceded to the request but before giving up his body, he expressed a last wish to be fulfilled. The last wish expressed by him was that he wanted to go on a pilgrimage to all the holy rivers of India. Indra thereafter, brought the water of all the holy rivers to Naimisharanya (supposed to have existed then somewhere near present day city of Lucknow) where Sage Dadhichi had set up his Ashram. Thereafter the Sage went into a deep meditation and released the life force from his body. The celestial kamadhenu calf then licked and removed all the flesh from his bones after which the Devas designed the 'Vajrayudha' (thunderbolt) from his spine and made numerous other weapons. The thunderbolt was used to kill the demon Vritra. Indra got back the kingdom and the water which was stolen by the demon was released for sustenance of all living beings of the earth. This was an act of supreme sacrifice of Sage Dadhichi for the survival and well-being of mankind.

Dhruba

King Uttanapada of the puranic lore had two wives namely Suniti and Suruchi. While Dhruba was born to Suniti, Uttama was born to Suruchi. Dhruba was elder to Uttama and was the natural heir to the throne. There being however, no love lost between the two queens, Suruchi, the step-mother was always envious of Dhruba. She once humiliated Dhruba when the latter, barely five years old, was sitting on the lap of his father on the throne. While forcefully removing Dhruba from his father's lap, she said with a lot of disdain, "Only God can allow you this privilege of sitting in the lap of the king."

Dhruba, the five-year-old child was determined to hear about his fate from the Lord himself. With that unfaltering resolve, he set out for the forest all alone. The divine sage Narada appeared before him and tried his best to dissuade himself from the extremely difficult path he had chosen for him at such a young age but it was of no avail. The sage, however, was impressed with Dhruba's iron will and determination and taught him how to practise penance in search of Lord Vishnu. The hymn that the sage Narada made Dhruba practise again and again was, "Om Namo Vasudevaya."(obeisance to Lord Vasudev). Dhruba, thereafter, sat for meditation with single minded concentration, devotion and determination. Lord Vishnu appeared before him but the child, to the surprise of the Lord, would not open his eyes as he was lost in a trance with Lord Vishnu's vision (as was taught to him by sage Narada). Eventually, the child opened his eyes but could not utter a single word. The Lord thereafter touched Dhruba's right cheek. Dhruba opened his eyes and poured out a beautiful stotra in 12 powerful verses praising the Lord. This in black and white is known as 'Dhruba Stuti' (Dhruba's Prayer). When the Lord asked him for a boon, he, having renounced all earthly desires simply asked for knowledge of a 'Stuti'(Prayer) with which the Lord can be praised and a life can be created in memory of the Lord for all time to come.

The Lord while granting him his fervent wish decreed that he on his death would become a celestial body which cannot be dissolved even by the 'Mahapralaya' (the great deluge). Dhruba returned to the kingdom, was warmly received by the family and attained the crown at the age of six. He ruled for many decades and after his death occupied the most revered seat of a celestial being - the pole star.

Eklavya

The character of Eklavya as depicted in 'Mahabharat' shows him as the son of 'Hiranyadhanus', the Chief of Nishads (hunter's community) who served under Jarasandh, the emperor of Magadh in his army as a general (Jarasandh was the most powerful king of the time). Right from his childhood, Eklavya had a passionate desire to be an outstanding archer. Once while hiding in the forest, he saw incognito Dronacharya teaching archery and various other skills of warfare to the Kaurava and Pandava princes. He collected the mud on which Drona had put his footsteps as a symbolic gesture of reverence for the knowledge of the great preceptor.

He erected a statue of his revered teacher under a tree and began practising archery for several years. While Dronacharya was moving in the same forest along with the Kaurava and Pandava brothers as his students, Arjuna, one of the Pandava brothers chanced to see a dog that was unable to bark as arrows had been shot all around his mouth. The construction was not a threat to the life of the dog; it merely prevented him from barking. Arjuna was amazed at such a bewildering skill in archery. Since Dronacharya had promised Arjuna that he would make him the most outstanding archer in the world, Arjuna shared his surprise with his preceptor and asked him how he was going to fulfil his promise.

Dronacharya felt distressed and wondered who could

be such a fine archer. He went around along with his disciples and chanced to meet Eklavya who came out from the point where he was practising archery and bowed to his guru. Drona asked Eklavya where and how he had learnt and mastered such superb archery skill. When Eklavya most respectfully pointed towards the earthen image of his guru which he had erected and before which he was practising archery, Drona demanded that guru dakshina will have to be paid if Eklavya was truly his disciple. Drona perceived in Eklavya a threat not only to the fulfillment of the promise he had made to Arjuna but as a future enemy of Hastinapur (as his father was serving as a general in the army of Magadh). He asked Eklavya to cut off his right thumb as guru dakshina.

Eklavya was fully aware of the consequences of such an action (he would no longer be able to practise archery) but instantly obliged Drona, his chosen preceptor by cutting off the thumb and presenting it without any grudge or grumble as guru dakshina to the former which was sudden and swift. This single act was a glowing testimony to the spirit of unparalleled devotion of a young disciple like Eklavya even though he belonged to a lower strata of the society.

It also demonstrates how mean and heartlessly cruel a Guru belonging to the upper strata of the society like Dronacharya could be towards a loyal, faithful and devoted disciple belonging to the lower strata. This is how Eklavya continues to inspire the admiration and veneration of succeeding generations. Today he is being worshipped in a temple at Khandsa village in Sector-37 of Gurugram city in Haryana State of India. According to folklore, this is the venue where he had cut off his right thumb to offer to his guru as guru dakshina.

(King) Indradyumna

His name is associated with the origin of Lord Jagannath at Puri. In all there are three legends which explain this origin. According to the first, after Lord Shree Krishna died at Dwarika, a piece of the bone of his chest could not be consumed by fire. The bone was thereafter tied to a twig and allowed to float away in the Arabian sea (Dwarika was located close to that sea). It landed at Neelachal on the East coast. King Indradyumna at that point of time was engaged in a penance at Neelachal to get a darshan of Lord Vishnu. The Lord appeared to him in a dream and directed him to get an image of Lord Vishnu carved out of 'Daru' (a log of wood), instal the bone which is tied to a twig and which has landed at East coast (Neelachal) and start the worship.

According to the second legend which finds place in the Vana Parva and Mushali Parva of 'Mahabharata' composed by Sudramuni Sarala Das of Odisha (15th century), Lord Krishna was shot by Jara Sabar and died. Before death he had entrusted the disposal of his body to Arjuna, his closest disciple. Arjuna failed to do so and caused into float in the Arabian sea. It came floating in the shape of a log of wood (Daru) and landed at the East coast (Neelachal). Indradyumna, son of Galmadhab, king of Sakalya island on the direction of the Lord in a dream engaged Viswakarma to get three images of Lord Jagannath, Lord Balabhadra and Devi Subhadra constructed out of the 'Daru'. The three images remained half-built and incomplete as the doors of the temple were indiscreetly opened by queen Gundicha contrary to the direction given by Viswakarma not to do so.

According to the third legend, Narada told Indradyumna that Lord Vishnu is being worshipped as Neelamadhab by Biswabasu, the hunter at Neelachaladham. Indradyumna sent Vidyapati, his Minister to enquire about it. Vidyapati enticed Lalita, daughter of Biswabasu and with her help got to know the site where Neelamadhab was being worshipped and went back to report to Indradyumna about the same. Thereafter, Indradyumna came to Neelachaldham, met Biswabasu at Charchika (Banki) (60 miles from Cuttack city) and struck bonds of friendship with him. He, however, failed to trace Neelmadhab who in the meanwhile had disappeared from the original place of his worship. Indradyumna got a message in the dream that the Lord is floating in the sea (Bay of Bengal) in the shape of a 'Daru' and he would like to reside in a temple if an image of him is built out of the 'Daru'.

Indradyumna got Viswakarma engaged for this purpose. Viswakarma agreed on the condition that the doors of the temple will not be opened before a prescribed date. Gundicha, the queen, however, got the doors opened out of anxiety as a stage was reached when no sound of construction could be heard from inside the temple. The three images of Lord Jagannath, Lord Balabhadra and Devi Subhadra were found in a half-built incomplete shape.

Years later, ruins of a temple with half-built images of the three deities were found by Chodaganga Dev of Ganga dynasty (1078-1147 AD). A Vaishnavite dedicated to Lord Jagannath, he started construction of Shree Jagannath temple at Puri which was completed by his son Anangabhim Dev 2 (1190-1198).

Jagadguru Adi Shankaracharya

Born in Kaladi on the bank of Periyar river (in Kerala State) to Namboodri parents in 8th century AD, Shankar took to sanyasa (penance) at a very young age (8). He was trained by Govindapada at Onkareswar on the bank of river Narmada, studied Vedas, Upanishads and Brahmasutra, travelled widely from Gujarat to Bengal to propagate his philosophy of Adwaita Vedanta through discourses and debates with other thinkers from both orthodox Hindu and heterodox non-Hindu traditions including Buddhism and defeated all his opponents in theological debates. As the legend surrounding his life goes, he had to enter a human body to learn about the origin of human species when he was confronted with such a baffling question by one of his opponents called Mundan Mishra, a noted Sanskrit and Vedic scholar, came back and defeated Mundan Mishra in the final round of the debate.

He is widely known for being an ardent and infallible exponent of the doctrine of Adwaita Vedanta and for his commentaries on 'Prasthantrayee' i.e. Vedic Canon (Brahmasutra), principal Upanishads (10 out of 108) and Srimad Bhagavad Geeta. Through these works, he argues in favour of unity of Atman and Nirguna Brahman (Brahman without attributes). Through such unity he defended the liberating of knowledge of the self, independent of the ritually oriented Mimansa School of Hinduism.

The principal tenets of his philosophy are: (a) moksha or nirvana (salvation) is possible, feasible and achievable in this life (b) Jeevamukti or liberation of the soul is the same as self-realisation i.e. awareness of one's own self and that of the universal spirit called 'Brahman' (c) Purity and steadfastness of mind achieved through yoga can act as an aid to have access to knowledge about moksha or nirvana (even though a yogic state of mind by itself is not enough).

Shankar's philosophy and theology had a profound impact on the doctrine of 'Adwaita Vedanta'. He founded four mutts (monasteries) in four different corners of India namely Puri, Sringeri, Dwarika and Badrinath. These monasteries are believed to have helped in the historical development, revival and propagation of 'Adwaita Vedanta'. Shankara had an unparalleled and unrivalled status in the tradition of 'Adwaita Vedanta'.

Authorship of over 300 texts is attributed to his name including commentaries (bhasya), original philosophical expositions (Prakaran Grantha) and poetry (Stotra). Amongst some of his most authentic works are:

- Brahmasutra Bhasya
- Commentaries on the 10 principal Upanishads
- Commentary on Sreemad Bhagavad Geeta
- Upadesha Shastri

There are at least fourteen known biographies of Jagat Guru Adi Shankaracharya's life.

(King) Jajati Keshari (1024-1040)

He was a king of the Soma dynasty, a devotee of Lord Shiva and builder of Lingaraj temple at Bhubaneswar. His other names are Chandihar, Mahashivagupta 3 and Jajati 2. As the story goes, his father Abhimanyu was killed in an internecine battle between Naghusa and Indraratha (995-1023 AD). Young Jajati thereafter escaped from his kingdom, went southward and joined the Chola army. He earned the goodwill of the Chola general due to his military skills and was instrumental in the attack of Koshala and victory of the Chola army in the battle that followed. Jajati became the king of Koshala in 1024 and was named as Mahashivagupta Jajati. From the copper inscription of Jatesinga Tungri, it appears that Jajati was the king of Kongada, Utkala and Koshala and was a source of terror to the kings of Karnata, Lata and Gurjara. He founded Jajatipur near Biraja kshetra on the bank of river Baitarani (one of the major rivers of Utkal/Odisha) and made it the capital of Utkal. As the legend goes further, he performed Dashaswamedha Yagya (sacrificial fire) and had invited 10,000 brahmins from Kanauj (now in Faizabad district of UP). Jajatipur became Yangyapur and later became Jajpur (one of the 30 districts of Odisha today). The remnants of the sacrificial fire tub and pillar can be seen at Jajpur even today. Jajati Keshari was the primary instrument for revival of Brahminism in Odisha. Jajpur is known for offering oblation to Gods and funeral cakes to forefathers. While Jajati Keshari patronised the construction of Lingaraj temple at Bhubaneswar, Kushaleswar temple at Anandpur (in Keonjhar district) and Chandeswar temple near Chilka (in Khurda district), his widow Rani Kolavati Sobhabati got the Brahmeswar temple constructed at Bhubaneswar. His son Udyot Keshari completed the construction of the Lingaraj temple at Bhubaneswar. After Jajatipur was devastated by the Chola invasion, Jajati got his capital shifted temporarily to Subarnapur (presently headquarters of Sonepur district called Subarnapur).

(King) Langula Narasimha Dev 1 (1239 - 1264 AD)
He is reported to be the most powerful king of the Chola dynasty and was the son of king Anangabhim Dev 3 (1211-1238) and Rani Kasturi Devi. He ascended the throne on 13.01.1239 after the death of his father. Both before and after his coronation, Odisha (then Utkal) was vulnerable to invasion from the Muslim rulers of the neighbouring State of Bengal. His father Anangabhim Dev 3 had no doubt successfully repulsed such invasion a number of times. Without waiting for the possibility of further invasion from the opponent's side, Langula Narasimha Dev built up a new strategy of attacking Bengal with strategic planning and preparation to take the enemy completely unaware and make them run for life. With that end in view, he commanded his army in 1243 AD towards Lucknowti and defeated administrator Tughril Tughan Khan near Bengal border at Katasin fort. He planned a second attack on Bengal in 1245 AD in which the Utkal army was commanded by his brother-in-law Paramardhi Deva (who had married Chandrika Devi, sister of the king).

He emerged victorious in this battle and occupied

both the divisions of Bengal on both sides of the river Ganges (namely Lakhnor, capital of Raj and Devkot, capital of Barendra). He attacked Bengal for the third time in 1247 AD, defeated Lakhtiyaruddin Yujbeg, administrator of Gaud and acquired a white elephant of inestimable value (even though tragically the general of Utkal army Paramardhi Deva was killed in this battle). The conflagration with Bengal continued till 1255 AD and there was cessation of hostilities only after the death of Yujbeg even though large parts of Bengal (Midnapore, Howrah and Hooghly) were annexed and became an integral part of Utkal. Through an unbroken and remarkable record of successes in battles with the neighbouring State of Bengal and beyond, he acquired vast fortunes and got the State treasury substantially enriched. He got a huge fort constructed at Raibania in Balasore (bordering Bengal) in 1245 AD.

The fort has a circumference of 8-miles and its boundary wall built with laterite stone was so strong that three horse-riding soldiers could effortlessly march thereon at the same time. He annexed Chhattisgarh in the West and built up an expansive and enemy-free rich Utkal by defeating the Kakatiya king in the South.

King Langula Narasimha Dev was a lover of fine art, literature and sculpture. Construction of the Sun temple at Konark on the eastern coast spread over 12 long years (1245-1256 AD) was the single most monumental contribution for which Langula Narasimha Deva is remembered today. He also patronised construction of Sikhareswar temple in Kapilas (15 kms from Dhenkanal) and a temple dedicated to Madangopal at Remuna (the temple which is known today as Ksheerachora Gopinath).

(Bhakta) Prahlada

Prahlada was born to Kayadu and Hiranyakashipu, a demon who had been granted a boon that he could not be killed by anything or anyone born from a living womb, neither by a man nor by an animal, neither during the day nor at night, neither indoors nor outdoors, neither on land nor in the air nor in water and by no man made weapon.

Prahlada, while being in his mother's womb, chanced to hear Narada chanting the glory of Lord Vishnu (His mother was passing through Narada Muni's ashram on her journey to some other place). After his birth, he continued reciting hymns dedicated to Lord Vishnu and was eventually initiated into worship of Lord Vishnu through continuous chanting of "Om Namo Bhagavate Vasudevay". His father being totally inimical to Lord Vishnu, did not at all relish the idea of his son singing the glory of Lord Vishnu and made all possible efforts to dissuade Prahlada from his ardent love and worship of Lord Vishnu. Having failed in all efforts to dissuade his son, the exasperated father made desperate attempts to kill him through poisoning, getting him trampled by elephants, throwing him into a river from a valley so that he drowns to death, putting him in the midst of deadly snakes and making him sit on the lap of Holika, sister of Hiranyakashipu on a pyre (the demon's sister was blessed that she would remain unhurt by fire) but Prahlada escaped unscathed by all these trials and tribulations with the gracious blessings of Lord Vishnu. Eventually, the demon struck a pillar with his sword in the palace and asked Prahlada "Show me where your Lord Vishnu is since you say that he is anywhere and everywhere." Lord Vishnu emerged from that pillar in the form of a man-lion (Narasimha), placed the demon on his thighs and tore him apart through his sharp claws at the entrance to his home at the twilight hour (dusk) (neither day nor night, neither indoors nor outdoors), thus nullifying the demon's boon of virtual invincibility and immortality. Prahlada eventually succeeded his father after the latter's death at the hands of Lord Vishnu and attained a place in Vaikuntha, the abode of Lord Vishnu.

Sadashiva Samantray

He was considered a jewel among architects and was the Minister and chief architect to the king of Utkal-Langula Narasimha Dev a1 (1239-64). He was also appointed by the king as the chief architect of Konark temple. He is reported to be a close friend of the king who admired his architectural skills. As the legend goes, he was so absorbed in the work of carving out an image from a piece of stone in that temple at an advanced stage of its construction that he did not notice the king himself standing behind him handing over a sweet betel made of betel leaf.

After the king entrusted him with the responsibility of being the chief architect of the Sun temple at Konark which, according to the king, was to excel in artistry and splendour all over the world, it was a formidable task for him to dig the foundation in the heart of the river Chandrabhaga (called Padmatola gorge) so that the temple resting on a chariot yoked to seven horses and driven by the Lord Sun himself could be successfully raised. As the legend goes further, he failed in successive attempts to dig the foundation in the middle of the river which was quite deep with very strong currents. The stones for filling up the gorge were being transported from Barunei hills of Khurda, stone bed of Kushabhadra river, from Satkosia gorge in Mahanadi river and from the stiff rocks on Brahmani river. Unfortunately every time the stones were put in the middle of the gorge, they would be washed away.

There was no doubt or dispute about the foundation being laid in the middle of the gorge as it was believed that deeper the foundation, stronger would be the temple. But instead of putting the stones from a side, they were straightaway being put in the middle and could not be sustained. That is how the foundation could not be laid for a long time. The chief architect felt sad and disappointed due to such failure and avoidable waste of time. As time was running out fast, out of frustration he left for a forest so that he would remain in obscurity and could not be taken to task by the king for his failure. As he was wandering in the forest broken hearted, he chanced to meet an old lady in a modest countryside cottage. He was hungry and requested her for food. The old lady served him hot gruel (a paste prepared from boiled rice which is a common dish served in poor households of Odisha). Out of extreme hunger and exhaustion, he was impatient and started eating from the middle of the plate and in the process, his fingers got scalded.

As he was suffering from acute pain, the old lady reminded him not to act foolishly like Sibei Santra, the Minister and chief architect to the king but to start taking the hot gruel from one side of the plate only to avoid getting scalded. He understood the implications of the statement, went back to Konark and started digging the foundation from a side of the gorge and not from the middle as before. This helped and the chief architect eventually emerged successful in laying a strong foundation.

He was given the title of 'Mahapatra' which gave him the position of a Minister to the king. As the chief architect of the Konark temple, he, under the patronage of the king, had mobilised 1200 masons/artisans/ sculptors from different parts of the State, finalised the design with the help of sculptors Bandhu Rath and Bishu Maharana (the latter was his chief advisor in construction of the temple) and had overseen the pace and progress of construction of the temple for 12 long years. He continues to be remembered for having the contributed to construction of this most wonderful legacy i.e. Konark temple (of 'Chola' dynasty which ruled the State for over a century), a unique piece of artistry, majesty, beauty and splendour.

Shuka Muni

A sage in Hinduism, he is the son of sage Vyasa, who composed 'Mahabharata'. Shuka Muni was the principal narrator of Bhagabat Purana by way of recitation of the glory of Lord Vishnu. He narrated to king Parikshit, the king of Hastinapur who was dying of the poison of Taskhyaka, the king of snakes (he was cursed to die as such by a sage whom he had insulted by putting a dead snake around his neck when the latter was lost in meditation).

According to the Hindu epic 'Mahabharata', after one hundred years of austerity by sage Vyas, Shuka (which in Sanskrit means a parrot) was churned out of a stick of fire. He was born with ascetic power with knowledge of the four Vedas dwelling within him. There are many other different stories about the birth of Shuka such as in Devi Bhagabat Purana, Skanda Purana etc. but they all agree on one point that Shuka was endowed with an extraordinary power of listening and remembering whatever he heard including the secret of immortality as revealed by Lord Shiva to Goddess Parvati, which demonstrates that he had superb receptivity and retentivity which are two most essential attributes for acquisition of knowledge.

According to Skanda Purana, sage Vyasa and his wife Vatika (alias Pinjala), daughter of sage Javali, had a son, Shuka who was capable of remembering and repeating every word that he listened to. The 'Mahabharata' recounts the story of Shuka being sent by Vyasa for training to King Janaka who was considered liberated (who had attained moksha) while still being a householder. Shuka studied under the Guru of the Gods called 'Vrihaspati' and sage Vyasa, his father. He was initiated into the path of liberation by Janaka.

There are stories about the phenomenal knowledge acquired by Shuka and how he surpassed his father in spiritual attainment. Once while following his son, Vyasa encountered a group of celestial nymphs (apsaras) who were bathing nude. Shuka's purity was so pristine that the nymphs did not consider him to be a distraction even though he was naked but covered themselves when Vyasa came in front of them.

(King) Sivi

Sivi is mentioned both as a kingdom as also the name of a king in the ancient Indian epic 'Mahabharata'. The king was well known for his truthfulness, magnanimity, kindness and compassion. According to 'Sivi Jataka', King Sivi (as Bodhisattwa) had ruled Siviratha with his capital at Aritthapur (Aristapura in Sanskrit). He is said to have donated both his eyes to a blind Brahmin. Chinese traveller Faxian records the scene of this story at So-ho-to (Swat), a country which is located to the south of Odiyana between Kabul and Indus rivers.

Sivi had a born instinct to instantly protect the poor and the weak even at the cost of his own life. The legend about his truthfulness and compassion goes as follows:

A pigeon who was being chased by a hawk took shelter with Sivi. The king could easily have killed the hawk, thereby protecting the helpless pigeon from his onslaughts but he refrained from doing so as by such killing he would have committed a grave sin and the sacrifice that he was then performing would have been devoid of merit. He was between the two horns of a dilemma and being unable to decide as to what was the right way. He decided to stand between the predator – the hawk and the helpless pigeon and begged the former to spare the helpless victim for anything in return. The hawk declined the offer, said that it was hungry, the pigeon was its normal and natural food and it was not interested in any other earthly object. However, he gave an alternative offer to the king to cut off an equal amount of flesh from his body as that of the pigeon, if he had such a magnanimous intent to save the life of the pigeon. The king agreed and chunks of flesh were removed from his body and put in the weighing balance to make it equal to that of the pigeon. Every time chunks of flesh were removed from his body and put in the weighing balance, they did not measure up to the weight of the pigeon. This eventually turned out to be a supreme test of munificence, magnanimity, truthfulness and compassion of the king and he emerged victorious. The hawk (a God in disguise) was struck by such an act of exemplary charity, mercy and large-heartedness, showered divine blessings on the king and departed.

Sapta Matrukas

In 'Brihat Samhita', Varaha Mihira, the noted astronomer of ancient India says that "Mothers are to be understood with cognisance of different major Hindu Gods corresponding to their names." They are associated with these Gods as their spouses or energies (Shakti) such as:

- Brahmani emerged from Brahma
- Vaishnavi from Vishnu
- Maheswari from Shiva
- Indrani from Indra
- Kaumari from Skanda

- Varahi from Varaha
- Chamunda from Devi Durga

In chapter 8 of 'Sridurgasaptasati' (seven hundred hymns dedicated to Goddess Durga), there is a vivid reference to how the energies of Brahma, Shiva, Kartikeya, Vishnu, Yagya Varaha, Narasimha and Indra came out of their bodies by the names of Brahmani, Maheswari, Kaumari, Vaishnavi, Varahi, Narasimhi and Aindri and fought the two demon brothers Shumbha and Nishumbha by the side of Goddess Durga. In Chapter 10 of Sridurgasaptasati tells us that when the demon Shumbha pointed out that Durga was fighting with the assistance of these female forces and not by herself alone, all the opulent manifestations entered her body and Durga fought, overpowered and killed the demon.

These are the Saptamatrukas to which a reference has been made by the author of 'Dharmapada' in verse no 39 of the English translated text. Jajati Keshari who had performed the Dashashwamedha Yagya (sacrificial fire) had got the images of the 'Sapta Matrukas' installed in the shape of huge statues at the venue of the Yagya (sacrificial fire) near Biraja Kshetra. According to the British archaeologist, Mr. Sterling, during the Muslim invasion of the 13th century the statues of all the Sapta Matrukas were uprooted and thrown inside Baitarani river. Some of them have subsequently been restored and placed inside the Biraja temple. Out of seven images, four were damaged beyond recognition by Kalapahada, the general of the Muslim army in the 16th century. Only three of the seven namely Chamunda (9' x 6'), Indrani (8' 8" x 5' 9") and Varahi (83" x 10") have been preserved. In 1866 Asst. Collector, Jajpur, Mr. Armstrong restored these three images out of garbage and preserved them in his official compound. These statues were built during 8th to 9th century AD.